CONTEMPORARY AMERICAN FICTION

WHY WE NEVER DANCED THE CHARLESTON

Harlan Greene lives in Charleston, South Carolina, where he is the archivist for the South Carolina Historical Society. This is his first novel.

WHY WE NEVER DANCED THE CHARLESTON

HARLAN GREENE

PENGUIN BOOKS

PENGUIN BOOKS

Viking Penguin Inc., 40 West 23rd Street, New York, New York 10010, U.S.A.
Penguin Books Ltd, Harmondsworth, Middlesex, England
Penguin Books Australia Ltd, Ringwood, Victoria, Australia
Penguin Books Canada Limited, 2801 John Street, Markham, Ontario, Canada L3R 1B4
Penguin Books (N.Z.) Ltd, 182–190 Wairau Road, Auckland 10, New Zealand

First published in the United States of America by St. Martin's Press, Inc., 1984
Published in Penguin Books 1985

LIBRARY OF CONGRESS CATALOGING IN PUBLICATION DATA
Greene, Harlan.
Why we never danced the Charleston.
Reprint. Originally published: New York:
St. Martin's/Marek, c1984.
I. Title.
[PS3557.R3799W5 1985]   813'.54   85-9387
ISBN 0 14 00.8218 2

Printed in the United States of America by
R. R. Donnelley & Sons Company, Harrisonburg, Virginia
Set in Goudy Old Style

For my parents:
By example and with love you taught me.
I owe you everything.

WHY WE NEVER DANCED THE CHARLESTON

PLEASE READ THIS NOTE FIRST

No matter who you are, whether you're a moon lover or not, I think you ought to know one or two things. You ought to know that this telling was not an easy thing for me; I had been putting it off for years—but not because I was lazy. Rather it was the reverse: I had grown old and anxious up here, waiting for the time, the signal, the opportunity; and they all came last night when for the first time in years I was called to the Battery.

I was not at all scared. My feet knew the way and they led me down the steps, over the vaguely lit streets and down the shadow-warped alleys—past those tall silent houses with their windows blanched bright in the moonlight. They stared out at me with the eyes of the blind. There was only the sound of my feet as I passed—nothing else; as if everyone else had been evacuated, I was by myself; I walked alone in a dreamer's unreality. Looking down at my hand, I saw every vein and wrinkle stand out; and every leaf, brick, and shadow stood out, too, limned, like a photograph, in an utter silver and black clarity. I could feel the rhythm of my pulse increase—not with exertion or fear, but with excitement. My years, like preconceptions, fell away, and in the moonlight I felt myself transforming so that I half expected, when I got down to the park, to see Hirsch there, leaning up against the sea wall, smiling that enigmatic smile of his, and looking at the light making patterns on the water as he had done on that first evening. Seeing me, he'd reach out and, spanning time, I'd reach back and we'd erase the fifty years in between.

When I arrived, I saw the park was still the same: the sea wall, the statues, the great archangel oaks and palmetto trees; in the damp and dimness, the two river lovers, the Cooper and the Ashley, felt but unseen; but mostly it was the eyes that convinced me, gleaming like Hirsch's with hunger and need. There were more than I had been used to

when I was younger; the number first surprised and then sad-
dened me. For in the cold light of the moon, I saw the faces
of many boys trapped in an anguish of lust and fear. I walked
by and looked at them; they looked away; I lost track count-
ing; and as the young will the old, they ignored me. All
seemed to be witnessing some ceremony as they waited for a
man in an automobile, a deliverer, to appear. I felt guilty for
what I had done to them, for the fate to which I had sen-
tenced them. I came back here.

I knew then what had to be done; I knew—but that
didn't make it any easier. It was rather like squinting into a
dark room, that trying to look into the future to see who you
would be, you who would find the notes I would write. I
wondered then as I do now what you would do with them. I
wondered if you would ignore them, brush them aside into a
trash pile; or would you burn them? Will you send my papers, along with all my books, to the Salvation Army? Or
will you read them and believe? Will you publish them for
others to read? It doesn't matter now, I suppose, for I have
learned what my Dah tried to teach me; she'd rock me in her
lap and brush my brow with her black hand and whisper,
"Shh; it be done; it be done"; so she would soothe me when
I cried over a broken toy. I have finally learned, Dah, and
will not worry.

But you, whoever you are, I issue you this warning; you
may not want to read any of this. You may not want to know
what happened to Hirsch Hess and Ned Grimke.

But you should, at least have the choice; I think you
have the right to decide for yourself. I'm sure you've been
aware of Hirsch and Ned, even if you've not known the reason or known it was their presence you were feeling. Having
come down the years and into the streets, their beliefs have
worked their way not just between the bricks, but into the
very consciousness of the city. Haven't you ever suddenly felt
a sadness in the air on warm spring evenings or tasted the
wistfulness or despair at the Battery? Haven't you wondered
why some names are never mentioned? Silence has slipped in
to cover their tracks, but they are still here. Hirsch and Ned

are trundling down the generations, trying to resolve themselves among the living.

I have to tell you one more thing—that no matter what you may have heard, I did not raise a hand against either of them. I'm not saying that I am innocent, however; for I did not raise a hand to prevent anything either. And for that— and not for what Miss Wragg claims—I am guilty.

The boys at the Battery don't believe this; in their versions it is I alone who cursed their city. I did not, believe me.

This is a story of two men who ruined themselves with love; the story of Hirsch and Ned—and me.

I was born in Savannah but spent most of my life in Charleston. Still this city never really accepted me. I was too nouveau, too outré for it; was born too far away to be taken seriously. I wish, though, that before I started on this journey, someone had told me that only Charlestonians themselves ever really arrive here. I would have gone back to Savannah, or done things differently. I see now that I was but a trespasser all along. I strayed down these streets in just the way I strayed into this story. But there is no one else who can tell it—or, at least, tell it correctly; and that is troublesome. I remember some things as clearly as my own name; others are fuzzy. So please bear with me. It is hard for an old man to begin at the beginning; to do that, I suppose I'll have to go back to Ned Grimke.

For I met Ned first. I met him years before I met Hirsch and long before any of us would ever turn up at the Battery. And even then, even that early, it was never Ned; it was always Ned Grimke. My family and I spoke and thought of him that way, as if he were too frail to stand alone, as if he had no character or personality not granted him by his family. He always did seem overwhelmed by them and shadowed by their past; but that was not very remarkable: many of my friends in Charleston and even Savannah were, to a degree. History haunted us all, especially those of us born in a sleepy old southern town that had Fort Sumter for a legacy. It rose up from the harbor to stain the sky. We could see it from our school windows, red in the morning. We were used to it, the symbol of the city, its epitome. We'd stare at it in awe and reverence while we said our morning prayers, as if the ruin was Zion, as if Sumter was the Olympus hovering over us. For God, we did not doubt, did dwell in Charleston; or the Lord of the lost cause did anyway. Savannah, we were taught, was not quite so bright a star in the constellation of southern cities. Charleston was the brightest, and many of

the boys I went to school with there bore holy names—
names that had gathered a romantic sound to them and had
garnered the prestige and patina of history—names like Lau-
rens and Middleton and Pinckney. It was not so for Ned.
There was a shame of sorts attached back then to being a
Grimke, a shame that was traced to two sisters of that name,
who in the early nineteenth century had believed that
women were equal to men; even more telling than that, they
had acknowledged a gentleman's—their father's—indiscre-
tion, and had accepted their half-black half-brother whole-
heartedly. There was something not so wonderful in being a
Grimke after that; and for their ideas, for their heresies, the
sisters had been forced north from the city.

Ned's first exclusion

Whoever you are who finds these notes, I wonder if you
will believe me if I tell you that their stigma remained all
those years later, and that the stain of their name was still
there when I was growing up. Something peculiar and unclean seemed to lurk even in its pronouncing; I think I can
remember, even as a child, how strange it sounded—as if it
were a word from another language. I remember a chill running down my spine as my mother checked my nails and
behind my ears and turned me over to my Dah to take me to
meet Ned Grimke.

"What's that?" I remember asking my mother.

"He is a boy, just like you," she said. "Take him, Dah."

"I don't want to go," I cried. I was scared by one of
those irrational fears in which childhood specializes.

"You must," my mother said; she kneeled beside me to
pat my hair. "And you must be kind to him and make him
feel welcome while he is here."

My Dah pressed my fingers together. Tightly. When she
did that I knew there was no chance. I looked at my mother
and waved as if going to Europe. She waved back. My Dah
took me down the street to meet Ned Grimke.

That was the beginning. It was the same year that Miss
Wragg first came here. I don't even recall if I liked Ned
Grimke at first: if we became friends, it was out of necessity,
for it seemed that summer that we were the only two boys in
the whole city.

Like every summer, heat had laid its seige and people refugeed as they had after Sumter; they went to Flat Rock, and to the mountains of North Carolina, as my family and I did usually. But the summer Ned and I first met, my grandmother lay ill and we could not leave. We were left in Charleston in the heat, and Grandmama lay gasping for breath, like a mullet out of water in a shuttered upstairs room. I tiptoed up to her doorway to listen to her inhales and her gasps as if they were the pronouncements of some deity. Dah would shoo me away if she saw me playing with my puppets in the doorway. I had several. The gendarme my grandmother had given me was the angel of death.

"He's coming for her," I told Dah.

"Boy," she warned, "don't even think those things."

She was scared of puppets and glass-eyed doll babies.

Often the doctor would appear. In a gloom that gripped the house as tensely as hands held in prayer, my parents spoke to him in whispers and interpreted every tiny change: was it a sign that the end was near, or did it signal a rally? They could not tell top from bottom in their weariness and so they felt cross and guilty in the heat. Lost in the shuffle of emotions, I slipped through people's fingers. Dah, my black nurse (and that was their generic name, Dah being an African word for mother, and one that best summed up their tragedy—that of those black women doomed to raise white babies), took me out for walks once in a while; but she spent most of her time with my sickly brother, Hal, who had been born in April. So I was free to wander the city.

I found Charleston a ghost town that summer—the houses hollow and the streets empty; the Charlestonians who could just went to cooler places before air-conditioning. The fact that we were left in town and were from Savannah was not lost on the other families. Grass grew up in the streets, and every afternoon the streetcar came by, depositing my father for his dinner, which we ate at three: cold potato salad, cutlets and shrimp, tomato sandwiches, okra or green beans. While we ate, the shutters of the nearby houses rattled like dice in the breeze and petals of overblown roses fell in green gardens abandoned to the ravages of creepers and ivy. The talk was sparse, mostly of my grandmother—what she had eaten that morning—and of the stranger's fever that had appeared here and there in the black sections of town. Passing a shack on the way home, my father said he had heard a scream and a black woman's malarial delirium. "New York," she had cried, "New York City." Later, nearly every afternoon, purple storm clouds came up from the sea and it rained and thunder boomed in the deserted streets; the old roof tiles were washed in a rainbow, a pigeonlike sheen. On Sunday, we could hear St. Michael's chimes throughout the whole city.

Time was a tunnel that summer, like the one I entered under the cool trees of Broad Street, to be passed through listlessly until September would bring its storms and October would arrive, leading people back to the city. It was halfway or so through that tunnel of summer (I think the hurricane lilies were out and wisteria was blooming again) when my mother came looking for me one morning; she examined me with a look of pride and inevitability. She sighed and suggested with a false brightness in her voice—as if she were suggesting something to which she had been forced to concur—that I go off and visit Ned Grimke.

There was no use resisting; Dah was the disciplinarian in our home and made me do everything my parents said; so we went, Dah and I, passing slowly down the streets, she matching her rhythm to mine. Going through the throbbing heat, we passed the hucksters calling out their wares, singing out for she-crab or "weggutubles" or shrimp; on a corner the ground-nut mauma dipped into a sweet grass basket and gave me a taste of her goods for free; and I thanked her.

"Thank *you*, white gentleman," she said.

They all tipped their hats out of respect for Dah—no mean feat, for some carried their wares on their heads. Though Standard Oil moved my father and us back and forth between Charleston and Savannah, the Charlestonians, all in all, considered us almost quality; Dah was attached to us and so she held the same ranking.

Finally we drew up in front of a dark green door, so dark it was almost black, and stopped. I lost my nerve. Both of us were scared, I think; both of us had heard tales of what went on behind these walls, but neither of us had ever entered the Confederate Home before that morning. It loomed up above us on Chalmers Street.

It seemed huge that day, the building, as it always did; and eternal; and gray, reaching up to eclipse the sky. Rust-stained and rain-streaked, the earthquake-bolted facade seemed clasped in some iron-clad bitterness; the three-storied back (the front is on Broad Street) rose like a medieval fortress, so abruptly, that I had never known until we summoned up our courage and entered that the building was arranged around an open courtyard, in the middle of which grew a huge and balanced cedar tree. Once we opened the door to the passageway, we could see the tree waving in front of us, green and dazzling, so that it seemed like sunlit water at the end of the dark walkway.

When we reached it, we looked up with eyes blinking: there were porches atop porches surrounding the courtyard; and on them, we could see, watering flowers in tin cans, or sitting in green wicker rocking chairs, or just pausing to look out over the railings, countless old ladies, looking like aged Juliets on their balconies.

"Do, Jedus," Dah moaned.

I said nothing.

They made sounds like bees humming. If they waited up there for their beaux, they waited in vain; for only death would ever come calling. I think they must have realized this, for all the ladies wore black, and it was that fact that frightened me most. To me, they looked like those ominous nuns I had seen circling in front of St. Mary's; my friend Dwin had told me that all nuns carried guns under their black habits, guns that had been issued to them by the Pope for each newborn Catholic baby.

I was scared of them and tried to call to my Dah but my mouth was dry; she stood rooted and all the ladies ignored us. We were mesmerized by them, so that we were surprised when Ned Grimke suddenly appeared.

We had heard him, without knowing that the sound heralded his coming—a funny scraping noise against wood, as if someone were coming downstairs dragging something metal, like a scythe, behind him. He was coming down one of the many ramshackle staircases that seemed to have been added as an afterthought to the building.

Because of the angle of the sun, he was half in and half out of the shadows; like a magician's saw, white light sliced him diagonally. He stood there on the bottom step, holding on to the newel post.

His head was in the sunlight; he was so blond it was almost blinding; and his pale skin was nearly the color of an albino. His eyes were the same blanched blue of the burnt-out sky that hot July morning. He seemed to gleam in the light, all thin elbows and knees. But he had a look my grandmother would have called "lively." We looked him up and down as if he were some vision; and I held onto Dah's hand. His shoes were peculiar: one was normal, while the other's sole was thicker by an inch or two; both were black and shiny.

Ned Grimke looked us over, too, surprise widening his eyes; he hung back, reaching for the banister, and tilted his head to one side, studying us.

Dah pried her fingers free from my moist hand and gently pushed me forward.

"Manners," she whispered.

"Hello," I responded, like her pet monkey.

Ned Grimke held tighter to the post and backed away.

With another prod from Dah, I held out my hand to shake, telling Ned my name and how my mother had sent us. He became solemn; he chewed his lip, clasped his own hand behind his back, and stared at mine, outstretched, as if it were something peculiar, a fish, I was offering.

He worked his jaw; his eyes drew light. He seemed to listen; then he reached out his hand and we shook; he bent from the waist in an old-fashioned bow, all the while saying not a thing.

"Cat got your tongue?" Dah asked.

He smiled, hung his head a little, and shyly shook it. His silence gave him a serious air. He blushed.

And no one moved or said a thing; we were suspended

there in the wilting silence, oppressive as the temperature. It came from all around, in waves, like heat; all you could hear were insects shrilling. Some folks said they were so loud that year they drove two colored people crazy.

"Where are your people, boy?" Dah asked gently.

Ned just turned his head to one side and whispered something to no one we could see; then he paused again and seemed to be listening. We were impressed by that—as if it was a sign of wisdom or maturity; he was unlike anyone I had met before and had roused my curiosity if not my sympathy. We knew (only because my mother had told us) that Ned was an orphan—or half a one: his mother was dead and his father had moved away after Ned's birth to Walhalla, South Carolina. I had never met an orphan before that I could remember and wondered if that thick shoe had anything to do with it—a mark of it, a badge maybe.

"Where are your aunts?" Dah asked.

Ned spoke to his shoulder; his eyes turned down, and Dah warned, "Boy, doan you make fun o' me. Where they be?"

We knew he was here visiting his father's two aunts, who lived in the Confederate Home. Those gaunt gray women, Azalea and Eola, though they did not like children, nevertheless insisted that Ned spend as much time as possible with them in his native city. This was not a wish—the thin old women did not give into whims—it was an abstract idea, inbred, against which there was no struggling. For, to them, Walhalla might just as well have been Africa. Azalea and Eola and all their family believed that true civilization existed only in Charleston and the low country, that thin strip of alluvial soil about forty miles in from the sea: plantation country—encompassing a few other populated areas— Richmond, Savannah, and by the grace of geography alone, New Orleans. Civilization existed only where it smelled of salt and seaweed; an almost underwater world in which moss dripped down from the trees; a damp and moist atmosphere that mildewed and moldered everything, one that had molded all of us—the Grimke sisters and all the other old ladies, Ned, my Dah, and me.

We stood there at the foot of the stairway, frozen in a tableau like wax figurines.

"Whooh!" Dah waved a handkerchief under her arm; she was sweating profusely. "I declare," she shook her head and muttered, "you too strange, boy." She looked along the walls of the porch—a chafed pink. There was no one around on the ground floor to appeal to; there were only the ladies on the porches hovering above us and we did not want to ask them anything. They were above us, like insects or chimney swifts swirling across the sky in the evening. There were steps leading up there, but they were useless. We knew the ladies were removed from us by more than mere height; they seemed as evanescent as light, as unearthly. They had been transported up there by their dreams; bereft, they were the wives, daughters, granddaughters, and great-nieces of those men who had fought for the Confederacy. Flesh may have withered; tints had changed from pink to lavender; but the unvanquished ideas of a vanished world still reigned here.

All of us children in Charleston knew of others, maiden aunts and spinster cousins, who had pressed their blossoms, shut them up and lovingly consigned them to where we found them on rainy days (in Bibles or albums), but they— the ladies of the Confederate Home—still clung to them like bridal bouquets, eternal Miss Havershams. They were vestal virgins.

They were not women, they were ideas; each obsessed with an individual past, each a small taper burning in memory:

"I am Richard Henry Duprée, cut down at First Manassas."

"I am my great-uncle Huger."

"I am chivalry."

We suspected them of taking such vows, and accused them of rituals and bizarre ceremonies. My Dah and I knew we had set foot on foreign soil when we entered; and we got no help at all from Ned Grimke. He hung there between the shadow and the light. "What do you think?" he asked himself out loud. "No! I won't!" he answered himself defiantly.

Dah was by now getting nervous—looking about for

whom Ned was talking to. She was always on the lookout for plat eye, ghosts, and zombies; I saw her touch the match she kept in her hair, knowing the sulfur would keep haints at bay. Ned spoke more to himself, and then with a lurching and not ungraceful movement, he came off the bottom step toward us.

Before we could do anything there was a movement on the stairs and Ned's own Dah appeared; she must have come down with him from the upcountry. She stood behind him and put her hands on his shoulders protectively. She was tall and thin, statuesque, part Indian perhaps; with her scarlet turban on her head she moved with great dignity. Then she mopped her hands on her white apron and, although she and my Dah had never met before, after dropping each other a curtsy, they immediately started speaking to each other in Gullah, their stark and grotesque patois.

She gave Ned a look that between those two, and those two alone, held a meaning. Each nodded slightly. The two black women moved off, speaking together.

Now Ned stood right in front of me. "Hello," he said.

"Who were you talking to?" I asked.

"A friend."

"Who? I didn't see anyone."

"He's tiny."

"Can I see him?"

He nodded.

I stood still, fascinated, as Ned pinched the air above his shoulders as if he were lifting something off that he then put in his other palm, offering it open and flat to me.

"It's Jervey."

He came over and lifted his palm to right in front of my eyes. "I don't see a thing."

"He's invisible." Ned then cocked his ears and listened. "Jervey says he's pleased to meet you."

"Oh." I was taken aback. "Can I hold him?"

Ned looked at his palm and then up at my eyes. He hesitated. "Okay."

I opened my hand next to his, our two index fingers

touching in a bridge. "Here he comes," Ned said. "Hold still."

I waited with baited breath. I could feel him. I said, "It tickles like a cricket!"

"He's dancing in your hand. But be careful," Ned worried; he dragged his foot and hovered nearby.

I was not about to admit that I didn't see anything. Jervey, in Ned's belief, seemed to be some sort of half man, half sprite, with wings.

"Where did he come from?" I asked.

"I found him."

"Where?"

"Over there." He pointed to a patch of deeper green under the cedar tree. "He may have belonged to one of the ladies."

"Why don't you ask?"

"Because then I'd have to give him back." He looked up at them. Ned was thoughtful about that for a while and said, "Jervey's tired."

"How do you know?"

"He told me."

"I didn't hear anything."

Ned snatched him quickly from my hand and put him in the hollow under his arm. "He likes it under there. He's sleeping."

"I'm gonna see if I can find me one." I ran over to the patch of clover and Ned followed me. With his hands, he lowered himself to the ground.

"What's wrong with your foot?" I asked. "Why's your shoe so big?"

Ned did not answer. He had turned to Jervey again, having wakened him up and transferred him to his ear. "You can't make me," he said.

I was poring through the clover and Dah called, "You git outta there, boy! Ain't I tell you not to play wit dem stink bugs?"

"I'm not, Dah."

But having issued her warning she paid no attention to

me. She and Ned's Dah were already thick as thieves.

All I found in the clover that morning was a dried-out cocoon—some shell an insect had left behind after molting; it was Jervey's, Ned told me; his carriage. "Give it to me," he demanded.

I did. "Why does he need a carriage when he has wings?"

"It's a secret," Ned said.

✳

"Do you think Jervey's real?" I asked my Dah as we walked home for dinner.

She thought about it for a while and touched the match in her hair again. "I seen stranger things," she confessed; "and he Dah done tole me . . ." She held off deliberately.

"What, Dah?"

I was limping like Ned, mimicking his uneasy shuffling gait.

She had not noticed it until then. "Doan you do that!" Dah cried. "Stop it." But I wouldn't. She told me she would give me one more warning, which is what she did. Old Dah was good to her word. When I wouldn't stop, she bottomed me. I stopped on the white-hot street.

"Come on, now," she coaxed.

"No; I be stoppin' right here."

"You ain't neither."

We argued in Gullah. I would lapse out of it and into English only when a white adult came near.

"You pull in your lower lip or some bird gonna perch on it," she warned, trying to get a smile from me.

But I would pay her no mind until she promised to tell me some of the tales Ned's Dah had told her—of cries in the swamp, of echoes under bridges, haints and boo daddies. It brought a chill to that summer heat. Fanning ourselves before dinner on the porch back home, she told me to stay away from Jervey. When I asked her why, she replied that things so tiny were liable to be mean.

So the next day, when I went back to the Confederate

Home, I was prepared. I was not about to play with Jervey, I informed Ned. "Dah told me he's mean."

"But he isn't." Ned seemed shocked at the idea.

"Dah says you've been witched."

"Uh uh!"

We argued that for days—until we actually fought. And of course I won. I was much bigger than Ned and he brought out the bully in me. After that we hated each other for a whole morning. Our Dahs made us apologize and our argument was forgotten; and so, oddly enough, was Jervey. Ned said he was shy and would not come out with me around; but I knew he was lying. I didn't say anything though. I think Ned Grimke was easily convinced; if I told him Jervey did not exist he would believe me. He'd believe anything, I discovered. That summer I convinced him that the moon was made of green cheese, nuns carried guns, and a man named Darwin had proved that black people were descended from monkeys. I had the opportunity to test out many of my theories. I'd believe them if I could convince Ned Grimke.

And I could. He was easy.

As the summer passed, we spent more and more time together. I liked being with him; for he was like an audience. He watched the puppet shows I staged in the backyard, shrieking out his glee as Harlequin and Pierrot acted out their destiny with Columbine. Sometimes, with dummies, I threw my voice and tried to speak without my lips moving.

Ned just watched, never asking to play with the puppets themselves, as if he knew I would say no or that he was not worthy. He sat like a pagan in church, impressed with the sheer panoply. And he *was* a pagan, for I saw him with a prayer book upside down in St. Michael's one Sunday. I pointed it out to my mother and she quieted me by saying that maybe he was not old enough to read; when I read to him from *Master Skylark* that next Monday, he was entranced. We acted it out with puppets (I had a Will Shakespeare). I think he started to worship me right then and there. One day, he said, when he grew up, he'd be me.

"You can't," I told him.

"Why?"

"Because I'm me."

Well, he'd be someone else, then, he said; but not Ned Grimke.

I advised him not to be a girl. He agreed.

We played everything—blindman's buff, mumblety-peg, Rebels and Yankees. I made Ned be the Yankee. He'd make a terrible face and act like Spoons Butler, Lincoln, or Sherman; I always won, being the good and saintly Robert E. Lee. We were watched over and sometimes even applauded by the old ladies.

Running him through with my saber one day, I demanded, "Die!"

Immediately he flopped down and lay gasping on the grass, pale and damp in the heat. I dropped an ant in his ear.

"That's not fair." He sat up.

Suddenly without any premonition of what I would do, I commanded him, "Touch me. Here."

"Where?"

"Between my legs." The silence was intense. There must not have been anyone watching that day for Ned reached out his fingers and I shivered as if I had been transported to winter.

Our games changed after that. There were no more Rebel and Yankee and we did not explore our town that summer; no, we explored our bodies. Each day we ran to a new hiding place in the Confederate Home building; when told to stay outside we played in the dust—or I did. Ned was content to watch me in the dimness that filtered down through the trees. He liked to touch me. In the green dream of the Confederate Home, we toyed with each other and made voodoo dolls to torture our enemies. We met often, and our days were like those dazzling dots of light that sifted through the branches of the cedar tree, that merged and danced and made designs about us. The summer seemed endless, each day undifferentiated, dizzy in heat and green. We were youngsters, our parents were adults; we had no idea we would ever grow up—we were a different species. It would be summer for us forever and we would always be children, the way there would always be fish in the sea. And though we did not mark them, there were changes all around us. The world went right on spinning. My grandmother got better and came down to breakfast one day, a little paler, perhaps, and a little weaker, but just as kind as ever; so the blinds went up and then they plunged immediately back down. Hal, my baby brother, developed a cough; his eyes rolled up in his head, he caught stranger's fever, and all I got to see was the tiny black box—smaller than my toy chest—and my mother's ruined face when she came back from the cemetery. Now there wasn't even a younger brother's toes to pull anymore so . . .

As the days came and went, the boy came over to my house or I went over to the Confederate Home. It was never Ned I visited. Always Ned Grimke.

"I want to touch you," I told him one day, and he lay there inert on his back.

"Okay," he said with his pants swooning around his feet.

Half reflected in his eyes, I could see the sky: the same color, the same continuity. He lay there like a paralyzed thing. He made no move as I passed my hand up and down over his white body. He did not object. His eyes did not register. They dreamed. It was the blankness there that made me do it. But I stopped as soon as he screamed.

✳

July melted into August as we lay under the trees; at night the racket of crickets kept us from sleeping. I remember there was a fire down on one of the cotton ships at the wharf; it burned to the water line, turning the whole city orange, as if summer had even ignited the sky, and the end of the world was coming. Dah was worried; she saw headless horses in the heavens; and as the fever peaked there was talk of a hooded figure, death, walking the city. She took the puppets away from me. Those were strange times. There had been springs of snow before, winters of heat, but that season to us was not the summer of fever; because of Miss Wragg it was the Summer of Ramses. She came to Charleston that year. It was her job to move the museum to its new rambling building.

Somehow my memory endows that scene with cotton candy and red, white, and blue bunting. Everyone left in town came to see, the old men to visit with their cronies and swap war stories; the old ladies because it was cultural; the young swains to offer help to this Massachusetts beauty. But she had no inclination to flirt; the young girls said she looked hard. Their beaux tried all the harder to impress Miss Wragg, who would not listen and gave orders like a man: brusquely. Notebook in hand, light hair swept in a bun, a pince-nez on her nose, she walked up and down the lines shooing us boys away like chickens, expecting perfect respect from everyone as if they had been born into her service. Her carriage erect, she was as chaste, as august, and as classic as a statue of Nefertiti; she was probably nineteen.

Our Dahs had escorted us. Ned was shy about his club foot and lowered his eyes as if the light stung them. He limped behind and I aped him; I saw a barefoot colored boy looking at Ned's odd shoe longingly. Ned Grimke hung back in the shadows of his Dah's full skirt while I tried to climb on my Dah's shoulders, like a monkey.

It took all day. Later my grandmother told me how upset she had been: she had thought the delirium was returning and she was back in Egypt, where she had gone on her wedding trip. "Imagine," she said, "looking out of your window in Montagu Street and seeing hundreds of men and boys and barking dogs, hearing a great rumbling." As the noise grew louder, the multitude approached, and then it was ghastly. The shape had cut off the sun and sent the street into shivers—into shadows that were so deep they seemed to be cast by time itself. It was the shape of history. Solemnly she witnessed it gliding past her window with huge unseeing eyes— the museum's cast of Ramses.

We followed it all the way to the deserted building whose wooden door-facing had to be removed to receive the monstrosity. Following it through that hole, summer seemed to disappear. Though still August, it was cool for a week; wisteria was still blooming.

My friend Swinton and his family came back to

Charleston; he was slightly older than me and somehow a cousin of the Grimkes. We played strip poker together during the year—he, Edwin, Hilary, and me. We knew what we were doing was wrong; but once we played it with Ned Grimke. He begged us to let him in, so what happened was his fault. Entirely.

He couldn't read his cards; all he could match were colors and shapes, so of course he lost; we played on until he stood undressed. I can see him still, white and skinny with only one shoe on.

"Take it off."

"I can't," he insisted. I told him that was cheating.

We were in a room with windows nailed shut and he was sweating; he started to untie his shoe, but had to stop. His fingers shook so. His shoe finally came free.

"Do, Jedus."

Ned Grimke's lip trembled and my eyes grew wide. I stared at his malformed foot as if it were the largest diamond in the world or an object of great beauty. The others left for dinner; I don't know how long I stared, oblivious of everything else; but I heard someone coming. I gathered up my clothes and ran half naked down the porch and into an old lady, who screamed. Ned tried to stand up but fell right over.

I did not go over that next day to visit Ned Grimke.

In fact, I saw Ned less and less after that and I don't think it was accidental; for I remember, soon after this, and probably because of it, that our Dahs had a real set-to; I remember them raising their voices at one another on one of those blue afternoons at the Confederate Home while they shelled pecans, and I lay with my head against a cool splintered column, somewhere between awake and sleeping.

"You!" Ned's Dah shouted at mine, flinging the bowl of pecans at her lap. "Take that boy of yours home. I dun see what he do; he be mean to my baby."

My Dah answered back, with what I don't know; I just recall the sound—they were like two marsh hens screeching. I was half asleep and Ned was sucking on sugar cane; my hands were already sticky with it and flies bothered me.

On and on they screamed; until Ned's Dah spit like a snake through her teeth and cursed me and my Dah and our family: I would never find peace or be happy. Flaking splinters of paint stuck like needles to my cheek as my Dah grabbed me up; she pulled me all the way home and threw me into the tub and liked to scrub the skin off me. I suppose she had to get the curse off. I thought she must have gone crazy. She muttered and said she would flail me alive and then pour pepper on my wounds if she ever caught me near the Confederate Home again or if I ever played with Ned Grimke.

I tried to reason with her; but her superstitions got the best of me. "I know he make you do dem things," Dah crooned. She took me from the tub, and with a towel and her love, she enveloped me. "He devil. Don't listen to what she say." She patted me dry. I had been fooled, she said, been used by that Ned Grimke.

After she dried and dressed me, she went off to do her chores. I followed her to the kitchen in the evening. It was taboo territory.

"Dah?" I whispered. "Dah, what you doin'?" Sometimes she entertained other colored people there. On a table in the center of the room, she had gathered together a small taper, a bleached animal skull, something evil-smelling stitched up in a red satchel, and a fish hook.

"Doan interrupt." She made me a coconspirator with her eyes and circled the candle three times with her fingers before lighting it.

She stood backward to it and mumbled words that had no meaning. "I get her . . . I get her . . ." she said to me. "That black bitch."

"How, Dah? With the fish hook?" She laughed and looked up to the heavens with the light catching her eyes and glinting off her gold teeth. "No, chile, just by believin'." She laughed at me.

She touched the fabric to the flame and an evil-smelling black smoke rose up to the ceiling.

That night as she put me to sleep, she repeatedly told me that I could not play with Ned. It was like an incantation she repeated as I lay ready for sleep; and she told me why; a cat had crawled into his crib before he had been christened. "Ned Dah she self, she once tole me."

"So what?" I asked, sitting up, and she turned dark ominous eyes on me. Hadn't I heard cats had nine lives? Fool! How did I suppose they got them? That cat had sucked Ned's soul like an oyster from its shell, clean out of his body. "You wanna be carried in some boy's pocket?" she asked me.

"No, Dah."

"Well, den lissen to me."

"But how can he do it, Dah?"

She sucked on her tooth for a while and inspiration came; Dah smiled beatifically. "That room in he shoe," she nodded, "yessir, it be a hole for soul-hiding."

I remembered. That foot of Ned's was a cloven hoof; I had seen it was so. Ned was the devil, she said, and I believed in her completely. I did not play with him, but I missed Ned Grimke. There was no one to give shows for, and no one to tell strange things to, to see if he believed them. I wondered if he even remembered me.

Sometimes I'd lay in bed and whisper, "The moon is made of green cheese . . . you are bad, Ned Grimke."

Summer was about over then, wearying itself out, burning holes in its fabric through its own intensity. In the evenings now, cool blue breezes thrilled the palmettos at the Battery. I don't know if Ned was hurt by my absence or not, but he had to go back to his father in Walhalla without a good-bye from me.

I saw him now and then over the next few years, when he came back to town to visit his aged aunts. He was only on the fringe of my crowd; I ran into him once with his cousin Swinton at Flat Rock, and on a few Easters at St. Michael's, and many years later, I saw him at the St. Cecilia Ball and some debutante parties. I had lost track of him, going back and forth to Savannah as I had done with my family. When I saw him I would stammer and blush and feel hot. I didn't much cotton to having him pop up all the time like a jack-in-the-box, to remind me of my childish cruelty. But Ned seemed bent on reminding me; he kept bringing it up all the time. At almost every opportunity, every time he had the chance, he'd ask, "Remember when we were kids together?" He'd say, "We were friends then, weren't we?"

He did this so many times that I could not help but wonder if he was not courting the same treatment from me now. If a bunch of us went off together on a weekend to someone's house in the country and some of us had to share a bed, Ned would invariably crawl into mine, talk about the puppet shows I used to hold, and then cuddle up like a cat with his head upside down and fall asleep; if he had an extra half of a sandwich, or a spare fifty cents for a drink, he'd share it with me.

People looked at us when we were together, and when he had gone off they'd say, "Well, you and Grimke there are certainly getting chummy." I tried to avoid him, but he kept coming back. His eyes, I noticed, still had that lively look they'd had as a child, but they were mocking now, as well; they were waiting, too, for what I could not tell. I can but ask, have you ever seen eyes that seem to say they know more about you than *you* do? It was with eyes like those that Ned looked at me; I avoided them; I avoided him.

He kept coming up to me. The closer he came, the further back I withdrew. He never seemed to realize this or complain of my behavior; instead he apologized for his own, giving the impression that a traveler must in misunderstanding the language and customs of a foreign country. He'd smile and say dumb things. He followed me around at parties. He laughed when I did and smiled at the same things that amused me—but he was always watching, looking out of the corner of his eye to see if I had realized it yet.

Had I? By raising his eyebrows he seemed to repeat with emphasis the question his eyes asked me.

They were daring me to take something up—to meet him somewhere. I will if you will, his glance seemed to say. After catching my eye, he'd move away recklessly.

So I was not at all looking forward to it when I heard that he would soon be moving permanently to Charleston.

"He's so immature," I told my friends. "He wants some growing up." They nodded. So there was no reason in the world to take him or anything he did seriously.

And I would not have—even after he moved back here—if I hadn't noticed him at a party once and suddenly wondered if he were queer.

Sometimes in the middle of the night my front bell will ring; often whoever's ringing it will lose courage and leave; but, at other times, one of them will be on my stoop, one of those boys Miss Wragg had spoken to, a boy come from the Battery, come to accuse me. One look is all I need; for the contortion of his face is peculiar. Have you ever seen righteousness mixed with fear? We study each other for a while.

And then I wave him in; and if he does come, he'll follow me back up the dark stairs reluctantly.

"Calm down," I'll say, switching on the light. "Don't worry." I had to tell the boy last night there was no reason to fear. I showed him. "See? They are just loose springs," I told him. "Those are not knives sticking out of the upholstery." He tried to smile; but, oh, once in here it was like a hothouse flower the way his fears bloomed: luxuriantly.

Finally, fortified with at least one drink, he relaxed a bit; and once he began he was hard pressed to stop; for like all of them who come here that boy believed in himself mightily. He had come here to accuse, but ended up in confessing. And some of what he said made me angry. For though it is the last half of the twentieth century, that boy last night still felt as sorry for himself as I did when I was his age. They don't know how easy they have it these days. They are gay, they say. They're not queer. They have evolved different words for different feelings; none of them have any idea how difficult it was for us. "Degenerate" or "invert" was the only way we were ever referred to, if we were referred to at all—and never in polite society. Is it any wonder then that we failed? Wasn't it inevitable that Hirsch and Ned and I would curse the city? God was different back then; it was before we enlightened Him and made the Lord into a kindly and avuncular figure. We felt more than guilty. We felt doomed, and were; we were so ignorant back then we didn't even know there was a "we." Each of us who grew up that way thought he was the only one of his kind in Charleston. I know I did.

For years I truly believed that the devil had chosen me for a reason of his own and made a separate little hell just for me. Laugh if you will—or feel sorry—but know that my thoughts back then, on the nights when I could not stop them, led me to others—to hair on my palms, death, hideous disease, insanity. Know that my thoughts led me out of my parents' house and down the street, back and forth, patrolling in front of Luden Renfrew's house on High Battery. I was drawn down there because he was the only one in Charleston I suspected of loving the moon as I did. I wanted to meet him—but I was scared to. There was no chance at all of running into him at the parties I attended, and where I saw my friends and Ned Grimke; he was not invited to these. He was not invited anywhere. My parents and their friends, when they deigned to speak of poor old Luden at all (Luden must have been at least fifty), spoke in horror, using the same tones of voice they reserved for uppity colored folk, pushy Hebrews, or Yankees. No one worth their social salt would set foot in his house, I was told. Sometimes, however, I longed to. I longed to see what sort of pleasure I could snatch from him before the jaws of hell opened up to claim me.

And I had some pretty lurid ideas, believe me. For the stories that came from Luden's house, along with an occasional midnight scream, were bloodcurdling. Everyone had a theory about what Luden did in private. Old Man Renfrew was a topic of conversation anyone could revert to when ladies were not around and everything else was too boring.

We were told all sorts of things; some said he conjured the devil; others made mention of violations too despicable to describe. But some of the plainer details were that Luden had been cut off by his family in Arkansas—that was no great loss for he owned his hometown and was the richest

man in something like seventeen counties. Seeking refine-
ment he had moved here to Charleston about ten years before, buying the old LaRue house, that fantastic pile of terra-
cotta, stone urns, and porticos on the Battery, immediately
expelling the dozen or so black families who had perched in
it, keeping goats in the hall and sending woodwork up the
chimney. Settling in, he soon set out to rise in society. He
joined St. Michael's Church. He gave liberally to the
U.D.C. and paid court to the highest families, and he met
with some success until his hand touched the wrong part of
someone's anatomy at a yacht club party. I believe there was
some talk about some servants of his quitting, too. From
then on, fewer and fewer RSVP'd his invitations; soon people crossed the street when they passed his house. If Robert
E. Lee could call Yankees "those people," then Charlestonians could call Luden "that man on the Battery." But that
didn't matter—not to me; many a night I walked up and
down the sea wall in front of his house like a sentry. I
smoked cigarette after cigarette, going hoarse and sending
signals with each struck match, each an SOS of sorts. Would
he help me? I wondered. I was ready to sell my birthright:
lentils would be a fair exchange for both my virginity and my
genealogy. It was a long trail that led me there, for the one
thing in the world I genuinely wanted was respectability.

I sincerely tried for it; I tried denying myself for years
and for a while it worked, but only because I didn't even
know what it was I was denying. Before I had discovered
Luden, I had no words to explain those desires that had
made me explore other boys' bodies as I had Ned's; the desires that led me on over the years, beyond strip poker, made
me bolder as I grew older, and drove me surprised and frightened into other men's arms at the Battery. For after I learned
of Luden and walked the sea wall, I saw that others were
doing the same thing. Strangers in town, they seemed to
have been drawn out into the moonlight, too. Had word
gotten out along the Eastern seaboard about him? Was it
instinctive in us? Had a map been handed out marking
Luden's house? We all gathered here, partaking in a ritual
that continues to this day—or night—at the Battery. And it

was from one of the strangers who took me to bed that I
finally found out the name for me. I had heard about the
love that dared not speak its name; and after what I heard, I
dared not show my face in Charleston. I was a victim of
moon lust, my stranger said; and he said that there were others in the world. (The world, I thought, okay; that's out
there. But how about here?) I was condemned like a vampire, he told me, to eternal darkness. I was nauseatingly
white and sluglike; I was a repulsive moonlit thing that
crawled out from under a rock and in to the evening. In a
word, I was queer. I was damned. I wanted to want a woman
with all my heart; I even tried, but couldn't go through with
it. And I couldn't confess that failing to anybody—not even
to my best friend Swinton, or to the others, Dwin and Hilary.

We boys had become pretty close over the years; we had
even banded together into a sort of club that we told no one
else about. We were not ashamed of it, or of ourselves, not
exactly; we were just cautious. For you see, we discussed
books, not women; took strolls on the beach and wrote
poems extolling the moon for her beauty. We felt safe and
warm with each other like kids under the covers at Christ-
mas; and as my desires grew more insistent I had had
thoughts of confessing them to my special friends; but I had
been afraid. I was so naive that I never suspected them and
they never suspected me. We lived in separate cells of fear. I
didn't think they could help; they were such good people,
especially Swinton; they could not be like me. Oh, I wanted
to be like them, and so told them nothing, terrified, as I was,
of losing their friendship. Then I saw Ned, and wondered if
he were not a moon lover like me.

We were in Hibernian Hall, that white Ionian temple
at the foot of Chalmers Street, at some ball, maybe even our
grandest of the season, the St. Cecilia; or it might have been
a debutante party. I can't remember that; but I can remember that it was a splendid evening. And what with all the
candles on the walls and the old gas-light fixtures above us
and some of the old gowns, you could almost believe it was
the nineteenth century. My father's business contacts, I sup-

pose, had gotten us in here. The Charlestonians did not like that in the least, and they blamed us for their poverty that made this a necessity. The musicians played only waltzes and reels and quadrilles, no modern themes; it was a ritual. The dancers could have been their own ancestors; times mixed; young men danced with old ladies. With the great oaken doors of the hall rolled shut, they could feel that there was nothing else transpiring in all the world. All that mattered was here. A young and foolish boy from Savannah could pretend that he belonged as well. And then, in a flash, in the whirr of the moment, it was all changed, shattered, like a champagne glass, with a sound that was shrill and disconcerting.

I had been standing along the wall watching the believers dance, trying not to be seen by anyone, when one of the managers silently whisked by. That usually meant some newspaperman was trying to break in to take photographs—a taboo thing by the by-laws of the Society—or some dowager had fainted, or a poor debutante had been caught smoking. That night, it was none of those things. The manager had not been quick enough to stop a couple from committing the unpardonable sin that has ever since been called "fast dancing."

Back then it was shocking. People nearly screamed as suddenly, without warning, as if having fits, Lucas Simons and Suzanne Pinckney broke into the Charleston, the dance that had been spawned on our street corners by colored children and would soon be mimicked across the country. As soon as Lucas and Suzanne began there arose a cry; other couples ran from the floor, holding their hands over their eyes, as if they were afraid they would be blinded by gazing at such deviltry. Lucas just smiled with his hands going wild on his knees and Suzanne reached for the heavens like a Jesus-crazed black lady. You almost expected to hear the screech of whistles or to see the police; but like reporters, they were not allowed in here. The believers had their own watchdogs of society. Men in evening dress quickly pushed past us and ushered the culprits off the dance floor; no one swooned, though many had seemed capable of it; there was a lot of fan snapping and tut-tutting among the old ladies. They issued dark prophecies and there were at least two fates sealed that evening—Suzanne and Lucas were expelled for their heresy; two positions in the elect became open in the St. Cecilia Society.

In the confusion of their dancing and being led away (I watched them as they walked out, heads up and wrists together, unrepentant and proud, as if being led to the guillotine), Lila Lesesne lowered the bodice of her gown and smiled at me. But I had had my fill of debutantes that night; and I was not going to volunteer for any extra duty if my name was not already on a dance card and no dowager sailed up to claim me for a visiting niece. I pretended not to see her. So Lila, undaunted, set her green eyes on Ned, and licked her teeth. He had been following me. I saw him blush bright red and immediately turn his eyes downward. He backed against the wall and tried to disappear. He was slightly taller than me, but still so bleached out, white as a skeleton, so skinny. He seemed out of place here; as if he had just dropped to earth and was not used to this atmosphere. Lila came his way; he gulped and blushed and chewed his lip. He looked to me to save him but I looked away. And that made me wonder if he were not like me. I started to blush too and suddenly was hot; I looked around to see if anyone noticed. As Lila spoke to Ned I slipped away to the punch bowl, and returned armed with two glasses. Ned looked up hopefully, but they weren't for him; people would think I was retrieving for some young lady, so I could wander about freely.

I walked around pretending I was looking for my girl; everyone I passed was whispering about Lucas and Suzanne. Would they leave town? Would they get married? The musicians started up a waltz; and after that, as if regrouping after a battle, people assembled for a Virginia reel. So they had survived; Charlestonians celebrated their own hardihood; it took more than one assault to destroy society. Lila Lesesne came my way with her arm linked through Winfield Huger's, and as they passed, I bowed and presented them with my two cups of punch. Winfield saluted, but Lila ignored me. I stood in the middle of the floor.

In a second, my friends came up; Hilary and Dwin came out of a corner looking like Jack Sprat and his wife, or Laurel and Hardy, Dwin thin and dried up, Hilary pink and pudgy with blond hair. They were always together.

"Where's Swinton?" I asked.

He was our best and we always gravitated to him; he was older than us by a few years; we felt somehow grander in his company. He was slim and dark; there was already some gray in his black hair and he had a refined face, a "French face," we said in Charleston, and an elegant body. We saw him across the room and he motioned us to silence.

The colored waiters in their white jackets were still whispering and flashing their white teeth as Swinton moved behind them and surreptitiously lifted a bottle of champagne from an ice bucket. He wiped it with a napkin and winked. He quickly put it under his coat, became solemn, and crossed the ballroom. In a flash I saw Ned marooned along the wall looking at us longingly with his blanched blue eyes. I looked away.

In the vestibule, I found my father helping my mother into her coat and I told them not to wait up. My mother blew me a kiss; we boys went out into the freezing night; and St. Michael's rang as we ran toward it, hooraying in victory as Swinton lifted the bottle. He held it up in tribute to the white church that loomed up at us like a wedding cake, tasteful and chaste under excesses of decorative white filigree. We went reeling and hallooing under the portico to Swinton's parents' house on Tradd Street. It *must* have been the St. Cecilia ball, for lights were on all over the city.

Up in his room, we loosened our ties and collars and removed our coats. We just lounged for a while, smoking cigarettes, feeling relieved not just from the constraints of our jackets and sashes and ties, but from all formality. It was all we drank I guess; Swinton wound up the gramophone and put on some records and silly Dwin pranced around in his underwear like a lady. The champagne was opened and we toasted. We raised our glasses, "To beauty!" Dwin fluttered his eyelids, pursed his lips, and moved his eyes and head and hands like Theda Bara in some movie. He blew kisses and we howled. Somehow it wasn't stupid; somehow it wasn't silly; it was exhilarating.

Dwin dropped down on the bed, with his legs jackknifing in the air; Hilary jumped on top of him. Swinton almost collapsed in laughter. And then I snapped down the window shades so quickly it sounded like a pistol shot. The gramophone stuck and Swinton lifted the needle; the silence was unsettling. Dwin and Hilary jumped off the bed as if it were on fire.

"We were only kidding, you know," Dwin said nervously.

Hilary chimed in, "We were only kidding."

I looked to Swinton. He was in medical school and had been in love once, the details of which he guarded zealously. He held up his hand and said, "Well, I guess now's the time to spill the beans." He was splendid. He was our best-looking.

"Well?" I asked.

He seemed to be thinking. He looked from Dwin to Hilary and back again; they were looking for cracks in his bedroom floor through which to disappear. Only a fool could not have seen that they were lovers—I mean, in love with the moon and each other. For how long had they hid it from themselves? How long could they hide it from us and their city?

"It's okay," Swinton said. "I know ya'll weren't kidding."

"We certainly were," Dwin insisted indignantly.

Hilary agreed.

"Oh, don't worry; admit it," Swinton said softly. He wound up the gramophone and poured the rest of the champagne. "Let's have a good time." He tossed his drink down and gagged when he saw his wristwatch. "Oh my God, it's late."

We got up and started undressing.

"Better get cracking, son," he said, tapping me on the

bottom. He got stuck and tripped getting out of his pants. "Hurry."

I don't think any of us really wanted to go out into the cold early morning; but it was such an ingrained habit as to be almost automatic. Before the Ball we had brought our old clothes over here to change into. It was as much of a ritual as the St. Cecilia itself; after the dance was over, and the ladies went home to discuss their beaux, it was time for us to discuss them when we went duck hunting.

I don't know. Perhaps you can go down the streets today and see this ritual still continuing—find boys along the curb, drunk and clinging to the lamp post, waiting for their rides to come. Ours came late that night—after two-thirty. We climbed like zombies into the back of Alfred's car, and drove what was considered fast in those days, careening through those funny Indian-named towns, occasionally grinding to a halt to leap out from the back rumble seat and pee on the great silent boles of the black oaks that twisted and lifted their mossed and massed branches up and away from the indignity. The night was cold and wakened us; the moon was spectral; we roared down the road like a rumor, singing spirituals, screaming in Gullah and drinking toasts to certain ladies.

It was about an hour later that we pulled up at the creek. In the plunging dark and chill, we rattled over the narrow plank dock, our laughter rising in the blackness. We went down to the batteaux; we rode over the inky water; we rode into the palpable blackness; and just our luck (or was it? I now think the other boys must have sensed our difference and allowed us our own company), by the time we reached our blind, we realized it would just be us four . . . Swinton, Dwin, Hilary, and me. We settled down quickly and wrapped ourselves in blankets.

No one spoke but Swinton. "I think we should organize a group," he said to us; "I think we should have regular meetings."

But we already belonged to so many different organizations: some to the St. Cecilia, all to the Chrestomatic, and others to the Sons of the Revolution; Hilary was in the St.

Andrew's, Dwin belonged to the League of Decency, and Swinton was a member of the Huguenot Society.

"There's always room for another," Swinton said; "and besides, I want to be president."

We accused him of empire building.

"Not at all," he disagreed.

"What would you call it?"

He answered too quickly for it to have been spontaneous. He must have been pondering it for quite a long while. "The Sons of Wisteria Society."

"What a peculiar name."

"What would be its purpose?"

"To understand ourselves; and to help others to." It sounded ominous to me.

Maybe it was because our hangovers were beginning to set in, or maybe it was because we ached with cold and dampness, but after that no one said a thing. Swinton produced his flask. He passed it and I pulled from it. I handed it back.

"This do make me amorous," Swinton said, laughing; "wants to make me go out hunting; and I don't mean ducks. How about you?" He looked to the other blinds and winked. Then he offered the flask to Dwin.

Dwin pursed his lips and said, "No, thank you." Disapproving, he said, "It wants to make you silly."

"Oh, shut up!" Swinton snapped.

"Don't talk to me that way!" Dwin said.

"You sound like an old maid," Swinton barked; Dwin made a sound and Swinton turned on him. "And speaking of that," he asked, "when are you going to get married? Huh? You're getting too old to be a bachelor." He was as quick as gun fire. "And how about you, Hilary?"

I had never seen him this way before. It was frightening.

"I haven't found anyone to ask," Hilary answered in a meek voice, and Swinton's laugh was ugly.

That shushed us; we sat silently in surprise, roused from sleep; fog eddied about us, touching us like Jacob's angel; the

water rippled, and the marsh grass swayed and stirred mysteriously. It seemed the sun would never rise.

From the other blinds we could hear tales of colored
women to be bought and whom to ask for and how much to
pay in certain alleys; we heard laughing. The boys in those
blinds were free to see themselves as the bloods of town—
and they did and they bragged of their bastards—they broke
out laughing, they, the cream of the aristocracy; snobbery
had nothing to do with sex, unless they committed themselves to what we couldn't, and settled down and got married. Oh, those stories. I tried not to hear them. Over the
years I had listened to my fill and had fabricated my own;
they were prerequisites to our standing. Like stigmata of my
shame, my palms started to sweat and Lila Lesesne's eyes
taunted me. I remembered Ned Grimke. Just then more
laughter rose up like a covey of quail on wing; hearing it in
the darkness made me depressed; and just like my feet were
in the frozen mud, my courage was sinking. Sound was all we
had (the moon had set); and in a bit but an unearthly stillness; there was nothing but our own breath in the darkness.
Swinton spoke in a new voice, abandoned by both courage
and whiskey. "I'm sorry I snapped," he said. "I owe you an
apology. But there's something I've been meaning to tell you
all," he continued. "It's about us," he stressed. "And them."
He jerked his head in the direction of the laughing.

"What about us?" Dwin asked.

"We're different."

"Oh, no we're not." Dwin cried. He was still angry with
Swinton. "We're just as good as they are; our families . . ."

"That's not what I mean."

Swinton's voice shook, like a singer at his first concert.
With nervousness, he lectured us for a while, and I'm glad it
was dark, for I would not have been able to meet his eye. I
could not believe what he was saying; it was as if he had
pinned back the top layer of my skin to reveal my hidden
secret. What he said smacked of medical textbooks he had
been reading. I flushed with shame and whiskey as that dread
revelatory word fell amidst us: I felt like vomiting.

We could invoke it and shape it, but speaking it was taboo; it would be telling. You have to understand that those years were simpler: Negroes were coloreds and Jews, Hebrews; and without words for such things, we felt they could not be realities. When Swinton said it, I felt as if a rifle went off in my head and I had been shot; no one could know; my senses spun and I gasped as if drowning. It summoned up visions of intestines and sounded like an unclean disease. I almost wet my pants when Swinton said "homosexuality." I was so terrified by it that it took me several minutes to realize that he was not pointing his finger at me. He was not singling anybody out. Instead, he said we were all in the same league; he himself was confessing! Meanwhile shame, like hot secretions, swept through me.

"No reason to get alarmed," he said; "we're not evil." He looked at our averted faces for support. "Look at me! What's wrong? We're not. Truly!" But we could not look at him.

It helped for Swinton to say those things, but it was useless. We all believed what we had been told, what each of us had learned years before from our Dahs, our preachers, our families. I trusted more in their words and ideas than my own feelings. I knew I was damned. I was convinced of it. My conscience resounded with things like "defiled" and "unclean"; terms sprang to my mind from King James's vocabulary. Like fish hooks, their ideas worked into me.

"We're just different," Swinton said; he caught himself on a note of hysteria and brought his voice down; soon he was relaxed and you'd have thought it was about the cut of our trousers he was speaking. "We're no worse than some; and much better than others," he said. "Just like every other minority."

But Dwin couldn't take it. He stabbed at the dirt and kept stabbing a stick in it; "It's not fair," he choked; he broke the stick in half and collapsed on his knees. I knew how he felt and would have comforted him but with what we had just heard, I was scared to touch him. He just wanted to be like everyone else; and was too much of a Charleston boy not to be scared of minorities.

"We have to admit it." Swinton was brave; "It's the truth; we don't have to be like Luden Renfrew"; Swinton would not give up. "We can have dignity."

Dwin was thumping his foot angrily by now. "Oh, shut up," he cried, leaping up to his feet. He planted a fist in Swinton's stomach; "I don't have to hear this"; he broke out of the blind and I could hear him crying.

Hilary rose up and went after him; "There, there," I heard him say, "that's all right, honey."

From the ensuing silence bloomed sounds that made me uneasy. I went into the reeds to throw up and ever since the combination of desire and sickness and repugnance, like the scent of a flower—wisteria—that blooms too sweetly, has been with me.

After a while, after Hilary and Dwin returned, Swinton continued; having with one toss thrown the whole ball of string in our laps, he found it expedient to now unravel its individual histories. He spoke lowly and steadily with a throb in his voice like a flame that would not be extinguished. "Look at the Greeks; look at Oscar Wilde; and Michelangelo; and Walt Whitman"; and he continued as he drank from the flask that some wished held hemlock. "Maybe even Socrates." For hours it seemed we wallowed in darkness, in awareness, and in misery.

The year before we had waited in the dark as Swinton told us stories of his grandfather, a drummer boy in the Civil War; how he had cried when his fingers were splintered by a minié ball, yet he did not stop playing. The same belief in something lost strained down the years and showed itself in him. Though outnumbered, he would not give up; and I got gooseflesh, when in the dark, I heard someone whistling "Dixie." I waited for the sun to rise; as it did rifles rang and death defiled the skies around us.

Around ten o'clock, Swinton led us back to the car, our eyes rimmed with weariness and blinking in the brightness. Walking back to the dock I felt lead-footed. I thought it was the wisdom, the word, the idea, but I guess I was wrong; I guess it was just the tiredness and lack of sleep after all; for I felt better the next morning.

I called Swinton a little hesitantly; he said he was glad
to hear from me and suggested that I come by that night;
when I got there he had succeeded in rounding up Hilary
and Dwin. Like a mimic, like an actor who had memorized
his cue and lines, I followed them through all the motions. I
didn't really know what the rest were thinking, but for myself I knew that since I was queer, the only thing that
awaited was suicide, loneliness, or disease. I was afraid to say
these things for fear of convincing others or being expelled
from their company. I was always to be nervous around
them, but I don't think they ever saw through me. With
another bottle of champagne, we drank toasts to each other;
we raised our glasses to the success of the Sons of Wisteria
Society and to Swinton, whom we nominated and elected
president. We spent the rest of that evening, if not actually
going down the streets canvassing, then at least ransacking
all our memories and impressions to see who else we could
invite to enroll as charter members. We met nearly every
night after that—not in one place—but going from bar to
bar. My skills, if not my outlook, improved with each drink.
I followed my friends everywhere. We were soon at the stage
of creating subcategories and finessing subtleties. Oh, to see
us you'd have thought we were as enthusiastic as amateur
bird watchers classifying newly spotted species. Beneath the
category of those who knew they were queer, we put (a)
those who were scared of it, (b) those who denied it, (c)
those we wanted to induct into the Sons of Wisteria. It was
inevitable, I guess, but in a while we evolved a special wish
category; messianically, we each put in a man we cherished,
one who would satisfy all our dreams. On reflex, Dwin and I
both filled that slot with Hirsch Hess; he was the most handsome man we knew. I saw him every day at the museum, and
had spent the spring before with him and Miss Wragg, riding
down the dirt roads of the low country. I had been too shy to
speak to him then, too much in awe of him and his beauty. I
had just watched him like a younger brother. Dwin, however, took every opportunity he could to leave work at Kerrison's and come by to visit the museum, just in the off chance

he could steal a glimpse of Hirsch in the nallway. We both ranked Hirsh high up in the reaches of beauty. Swinton did not disagree with us (nor did Hilary), but he said that we were fools not to realize sure Hirsh Hess was queer; but to us, to me anyway, it did not seem possible, overwhelmed as we were by his extravagant maleness, his darkness and intensity.

But that's just what convinced Swinton. He said, "It's just like the Greeks." We, however, did not know our history. We thought Hirsch was too good-looking to be one of us.

So we argued over him and other things; we gossiped and suggested others to membership; and though I did not forget him, I never once mentioned Ned Grimke, for I didn't want to be part of the Sons of Wisteria if Ned was; and so for a while I was free of him. From bar to bar we went, whispering together like conspirators, giggling like schoolgirls, rootless as gypsies. I remember the night that Swinton called us together and tapped excitedly with his finger on a glass. "Guess what?" he asked.

"Did you find out about Hirsch Hess?" I asked; "or Reverend Simkins?"

"Better." He could hardly keep his voice down. He nearly crowed. "There's a bar for us."

"Us?"

"The Sons of Wisteria."

Dwin was disbelieving. "What do you mean?"

Swinton started to answer in rapture; but Dwin quieted him. "Shh," he warned, "folks'll hear."

"Can you take us there?" I asked.

Swinton nodded, a smile splitting his face.

"When?"

"Now."

We looked at each other in happiness and, suddenly, in fear. "But what if we're seen?" Dwin asked in horror.

"But who'll be seeing us but queers?" came from Hilary.

"I knew I liked you for some reason other than your good looks," Dwin answered him. "I'll buy you a drink."

"There?"

"Yes!"

We got up right away and reached for our coats. It was to be the first of I don't know how many of our nights at Chicco's Peacock Alley.

Swinton led the way and we followed. I can still hear the rush of our feet, the patter of our hearts; we were too excited and we moved too quickly to speak. All our other journeys here would be made at night; we would always need the cover of evening.

We ran through the slatted moonlight of the Market, spooking its stray cats and rats, prostitutes and thieves. Swinton turned a corner and stopped so abruptly that we almost ran into him. Catching our breath, we drew up in front of the Peacock Alley.

There it stood, in French Ending Street, in a building that has long since disappeared. It loomed up cool and ghostly in the moonlight. An Egyptian sun rose in the pressed metal gable; ankhs made holes in the shutters; and a marble slab declaring "Young America. 1866." was bracketed over the doorway.

"What does it mean?" Dwin asked.

Swinton shrugged. No one understood its evolution, its architecture, or its meaning. But we did not question. We approached. For such as it was, it was ours, and history's; for the first time in Charleston there was a place for us queers besides Old Man Renfrew's house, parked cars, Baptist hells, and the Battery. We were curious, to say the least. But, like savages come upon a ruined temple in the jungle, we approached the doorway cautiously.

We stopped when we heard laughter ring out from behind the door and ricochet down the streets. Like bat wings the echos beat off the somber walls of the warehouses, winding down like the final notes of a plaintive symphony.

We squinted. Emerging from the dimness, the design on

the door made us jump: a peacock with a spread thousand-eyed tail, all of the eyes watching.

"It wasn't here last time," Swinton said; "or if it was, I sure didn't notice it." He coughed into his hand and rattled the door knob; one of the peacock's eyes blinked; it was a human eye, bloodshot, staring. The door opened slowly.

Swinton was the first and we followed him in single file as if he were leading us down into an Egyptian tomb. Entering the alleylike hall, we saw hundreds of eyes reflecting back and forth in mirrors, into eternity. The passageway was tiled with tiny tilted mirrored squares, all of different sizes and shapes. Eyes had been painted on some of them. And in the confusion of entering, other boys seemed to be rushing at us.

We made our excuses until we realized, to our chagrin, that we were apologizing to ourselves.

There was a laugh behind us, and we all turned around to see.

To the right of the door, on a high stool, sat a dwarf with the pushed-in face of a deflated rubber squeeze toy. His smile deformed it even more. He was rubbing his hands together on his knees. It had been his laugh we had heard in the street. He was four feet tall and nearly bald, with just a whisp of blond hair curled atop his head; he wore old coveralls with no shirt, so that his shoulder blades stuck out peculiarly.

"Good evening," he said in a nasal squeaky voice.

"Hi," Swinton said, extending his hand. "Remember me? I'm back." They shook repeatedly.

"Yes, I see." The midget let go of Swinton's hand. His eyes flicked to each of us; like a cat's they were yellow-green; and like a cat's, too, there was an intelligence behind them, but you had no clue to what the creature could be thinking.

Swinton told the dwarf our names as we came up, one by one, and as if he were royalty, the midget gave us his hand to touch. When my turn came I almost shuddered: he was cold and pink and moist to the touch. He asked each of us who our parents were, where we lived, and what we did for a profession. It was like an inquisition. We told him the truth; we would have confessed to anything.

I told him I worked at the museum.

"So you must know our Mr. Hess."

I confessed with wonder that I did. "Do you?"

The midget smiled. "He's one of my loveliest," he said as if he had dozens of others for the choosing.

With the garish light of the entry, all I needed was a whiff of sulfur to convince me that I had come upon the gates of hell and Old Scratch himself was there to greet me. He held us in his gaze for another minute as though he were weighing our destinies. Then he nodded and spread his arms. "Welcome; I hope ya'll have a good time. Have your first one on me." He smiled and waved us on down the hall.

We thanked him and proceeded in the indicated direction.

"Who was that?" all of us demanded of Swinton at once.

"The owner," he whispered. "His name is Chicco."

"Chicco who?"

He shrugged, and told us all that he knew. Chicco lived off on Mazyck Street in an attic of a whorehouse. There was a big black man who lived there, too, who sometimes called him "Chick Pea."

Dwin laughed. "Shh! Don't make fun of him," Swinton warned; "he can be plenty mean." He lowered his voice conspiratorially. Chicco was like God in the mirror, Swinton said, or Jehovah in reverse—quick to anger and slow to reconcile. He held grudges forever, so you did not treat him lightly. "Be nice," he stressed; "and don't look back."

We didn't. We entered an arched brick doorway.

The bar itself was now in front of us, a tap room of dark rubbed wood like something from the eighteenth century. The bartender, with plucked eyebrows and hardly any hair, looked like a mannequin in some dress-shop window that someone had snatched wigless. "Hello," it said in a high reedy voice. "What'll it be?" Fixing our drinks it flitted back and forth between man and woman as if both were living in its body. He was like no one we had ever seen.

We drank, looking around, trying not to appear too naive.

But it was too dark to see. The place was lit with a few dim bulbs and with candles in wine bottles on the tables, some out, some guttering.

We entered the main room through a wide arch and down a few steps to our left; its walls were of brick, with a great fireplace along the left wall where a hot, though neglected fire gleamed. We warmed our hands for a moment. Great hewn beams supported the ceiling. A dozen or so wooden tables spread throughout the room, with split bottom chairs around them; the tables we could see as we passed were all scarred with cigarette burns and gouged out with initials. There was a higher level across from us with what looked like a dance floor, and a few tables, chairs, and a forlorn piano stood under half-sized, smudged windows.

"There's music on weekends," Swinton said.

We clustered around him in the low and smoky dimness and looked around more bravely. Across from us near the small dance floor I thought I recognized someone.

The man was in the process of examining us. I felt his glance like a caress. It was like stepping into a steam room here.

I felt dizzy as pitch-black eyes, set in the fiercest though handsomest face I had ever seen, turned on me.

"It's Hirsch Hess," I whispered, nudging Swinton.

"Where? Where is he?" Dwin's voice was urgent. He was on tiptoes craning to see.

"I don't see him."

"There!"

"Where? Oh!"

Hirsch had turned away to get a cigarette from the pocket of his coat, which hung on a chair behind him. Slowly his face reappeared—first in profile—the curve of his cheek, as time stopped for us and a match flared.

Hirsch Hess seemed to be made of grander stuff than we; he was larger than life, dramatic. Dwin and I had once compared him to Michelangelo's *David*, of which we had photographs, and that Swinton on his tour of Italy had actually seen. But coming upon him in the Alley, we realized how foolish we had been, for Hirsch's features were not perfect; they were better than that, for they were flawed with a wonderful vulnerability. His features were strong and massive, yet their fineness of line and proportion restrained what otherwise might have been an overpowering virility. As he examined us, we watched him as one would a sunset, a spectacle, or a tragedy.

Settling back on his seat, he was finishing his examination of us, going over us one by one. I saw in his eyes that he recognized me, but rather than please him it seemed to make him angry.

I tried to call out but my throat was too dry. My voice cracked.

He looked at me disgustedly.

All of us hung there while Hirsch pondered. He did not smile. He shrugged his shoulders with a sense of the inevitable, and gave in. He nodded and stood up and pulled up chairs for us. We crossed the room to sit with him. After a welter of outstretched arms and shy introductions, Dwin said, "I've always wanted to meet you."

After this brief spurt of talk, silence fell; we were off to a bad start and everyone looked at me to keep the conversation going.

But I hardly knew him; I only saw him at work in the mornings, and then we rarely spoke. I had been too shy to approach him that spring before, when Miss Wragg and he and I went down on her missions into the low country. He usually spent all his time in her office; and after Miss Wragg hired me as puppeteer, he would come every once in a while to the children's hall, and stand in the back and watch as I acted out fairy tales with Punch and Judy, teaching kids the magic of thank you and the mystery of please. Hirsch would just stand there against the door frame, his arms crossed against his chest, eyeing me cynically. In his eyes, we all were children.

You practice a lot in mirrors when you're a puppeteer; one day I was watching Punch kiss Judy and had no idea that anyone else was there when I heard laughter. Hirsch was in the back of the hall looking down at me. "Miss Wragg wouldn't like that," he said. "No fraternizing among the staff." He made a joke about a wooden pecker; I winced at that vulgarity and when I spoke, I still had the swazzle in my mouth, that bamboo and leather reed that you use to make Punch sound the way he does, and Hirsch laughed even more. He was making fun of me.

And now sitting there in the bar, his look was one of defiance. He seemed to be daring us to speak. Only Swinton did, asking, "How long have you been coming here?"

"How long?" Hirsch laughed with a sad, seemingly unwilling cynicism. "Since I was . . ." he stopped and looked at Swinton. "Seventeen."

We were impressed, exchanging glances. For we were, at the time, between twenty-two and twenty-three. Swinton at the most was twenty-seven; Hirsch was the same age as the rest of us. He had beaten us here by five years. He had given up what we still clung to that long ago. We were ashamed by our naiveté.

It would have been something to see: like the child of Israel that he was, Hirsch must have entered the doors of that bar as though entering the Promised Land, expecting delivery. But he had crossed no River Jordan—not on that night or any of the following. "When I got in here," he said, "Old Man Renfrew, just like a spider, was sitting over there waiting." He spoke quite blandly about it, not seeing how shocked we were. "That old man will do anything."

"Like what?" we wanted to ask, but dared not.

"But he didn't stop me. Oh no!" He told us he came back to the Alley the next night; and the next and the next; hardly an evening could pass after that with Hirsch not making an appearance at the Alley. "I live here," he said; Chicco obviously encouraged it, and for good reason. Hirsch was good for business; a kind of bait. We eventually realized that attention always turned to Hirsch when he came in; he was the genius of the place: the air became charged when he paraded into the Peacock Alley. All eyes were on him when we sat with him; and although the table was littered with glasses—tributes from the management, sad old men, his admirers—Hirsch was not drunk. The glasses surrounded him like a semicircle of trophies. I think his capacity for drink must have equaled his for suffering.

He drained another glass and thumped it down on the table; he looked both lost and triumphant. He snapped his fingers and the bartender appeared. "Another round," he said, flinging out some bills. We thanked him and took our drinks, eyeing him over their rims. And all we would ever learn of him was summed up right then that evening. Hirsch, we could see, drank everything to the bitter lees, savoring them. He downed his drink and put it back on the table. We drank ours slowly. Nothing was as real for us as it was for Hirsch.

"Excuse me." He got up and wiped his lips on the back of his hand. "I'll be right back."

Like hypnotized victims, we kept our eyes on Hirsch. Chicco came into the bar and stood in the archway. Hirsch went up to him, and we could see the midget offer him money, which was fanning out between his fingers like a green bouquet.

While Hirsch was away, there was a change of atmosphere at our table. We all breathed in deeply, not relieved, just released from the nervousness he evoked in us. And there was pure envy. Our groins were swollen and we crossed our legs. We were dazed. *Seventeen.* We tried to imagine it, but couldn't.

At seventeen, he discovered the Alley; before then we would see him on late summer evenings. When work was over and the dishes done, Hirsch would spend time with his parents, sitting with them on their porch on Mazyck Street, watching people pass by, speaking in low tones with their syllables dissevered, or softly laughing; whores passed their way like pillars of fire all aflame in their satin finery. Like a medieval procession there also came the dubious, the jealous, and those seeking release, on their way to the witch doctor who lived next door to the Hesses, going for a fetish. For Mr. and Mrs. Hess lived in the colored section of town, a section we visited rarely except when we were lowering ourselves. Mazyck Street seemed to recognize this; once being swampy and malarial, it was now always puddled after rain: the houses leaned at crazy angles and the ground was sinking. Some of our friends found relief in the colored whorehouses nearby, but others—we good boys banished from heaven—only went down that street on a dare or on a shortcut to the west side of the city. So the Hesses saw us passing too; like souls lost in limbo, we did not say hello or good evening, nor did they. On into the lengthening night, Mr. and Mrs. Hess would sit, rocking, silent, watching the people pass; Hirsch turned uneasily in his seat. It was his parents who held him here. Though the moonlight made him restless and he ached with the unsung beauty of his flesh, he knew there was no escaping.

"What do you know of him?" I had asked Swinton once as we passed by.

"Hirsch Hess?" he said, looking at him. "He's Hebrew; and sometimes I see his father on King Street." Swinton clucked his tongue and his eyes lingered on the bulges of Hirsch's body. "He looks intelligent, too."

Later when we worked together at the museum, more and more people would ask me what I knew of him. I would not have much to say, for we worked in different departments and after spring I saw him only in the mornings over coffee. He spent most of his time with Miss Wragg, who had hired him as her assistant at about the same time she had taken me on as puppeteer. With the aid of Punch and Judy, it was my lot to introduce the kids of Charleston County to the world of ideas.

Hirsch needed no introduction; he lived in the world of ideas, we would discover shortly. He drank of them deeply. We saw he had fascinations. We would witness his flings; but I think what Hirsch really had a penchant for was the grotesque. He was pulled, not like a moth, but more like a martyr, to the flame; to things gas-green from the past. Not his; and certainly not Charleston's. It was his parents' past that fascinated Hirsch; you could tell as soon as they opened their mouths that they were not of us. One word and you knew they were from the old country.

If those poor people were alive today, I shouldn't wonder but that there'd be an article about them in the newspaper. They'd even be held up as heroic. But back then we were ashamed of them. We relegated Mr. and Mrs. Hess to oblivion on their cold and decaying side street; for they seemed too peculiar to befriend, too touched and tainted by their history.

Except on her porch, withdrawn, frightened, watching, hardly anyone in town ever saw Hirsch's mother. Mrs. Hess was short and stark, her features dangerous and her eyes as bright blue and baleful as a gypsy's. In Poland, where she was born, she had been a pretty young woman of some standing when she married a farmer's son. It was rumored—no one seemed to know for sure—that she spoke French and had studied at a university. But then, in a pogrom, in the fury unleashed by the cry of a crazed peasant woman at Passover, "The Jews murdered my son," in the wave of murder in the streets, with blood on the doorpost, and the destruction, her pretensions were trampled. Her shame of being a Jewess disallowed them. And whatever remained must have been undone by her being Jewish in Charleston, where the natives looked down on that as an unfortunate, though irrevocable, birth defect or deformity. I suppose the other Jews in town saw the Hesses as something unpleasant and unnerving too.

Mrs. Hess would not leave the house if she could help it. She could not find her way around the twisted streets of Charleston and she would not ask; she was not proud, she was suspicious. Once she accused the grocer of poisoning her celery. She often told Hirsch that he could not trust anyone.

She may not have been well known, but everyone in town was familiar with her husband. We all knew that Mr. Hess repaired shoes on King Street in a ramshackle building he called the Cat Sole New Shoery. It had a big plate glass window of two panes, over which two smiling black cats and his business name were horseshoed. Through the grimy windows you could see the old flecked wooden booths where you could sit and puzzle over yesterday's Yiddish paper while your shoes were shined by one of Mr. Hess's colored employees. He had inherited them when someone had sold him the business soon after his arrival. He had gone south when he was told that there had been Jews in Charleston for centuries. But assimilation was the key in Charleston; and the Hesses, with their manners, their customs, their speech and grisly history, were like gristle—something too tough for digesting. It was better to ignore him and take your shoes instead to the Greeks down the street. Everyone knew he catered to the best Charleston families. And everyone who did pass Mr. Hess by, or who walked King Street in the late afternoon or evening, would have been startled at least once, I am sure, at seeing him in his particular booth. The pogrom had affected him, too. Every afternoon he'd sit there, his eyeglasses drawn up above his eyes to rest on his forehead, his paper in his lap, staring. How could life have brought him here to this hot and hostile gentile city? his blank stare seemed to demand. And now that he was here, he seemed incapable of leaving, as if in that one flight, that one escape from the pogrom, he had used up all his energy. He was a big and rambling man; a grayness like dust had settled in his face, a slackly hawkish one that was perpetually befuddled and rank with a three-day beard and mystery. He shook his head in bafflement. Sometimes he'd stand outside on the street or lean against his building. As children, we took to running away with crossed fingers just to avoid his cooties. All our Dahs used him; he became the bogeyman and the wandering Jew of many a Charleston child's mythology. What was there in Hirsch's splendidness to connect him with his parents?

That is what we wondered when we saw him that night and all those that followed in the Alley. Hirsch was so gloriously fine, so audaciously handsome. If Hirsch had been religious, he could have spent his whole life just witnessing—serving as a testament to God's glory and wisdom. So handsome was he that it—and you must think of Hirsch's beauty as an entity to itself—was a much discussed thing in Charleston, and not just among us boys at the Peacock Alley. For I remember Miss Wragg introducing Hirsch to Miss Willis ("Miss Priss" we called her) and she, a spinster, felt in her purse for her handkerchief and cried into it as if in a sneeze, "I never thought I'd desire again!" She looked at him (we in the distance who overheard broke out laughing), but Hirsch ignored her and went right past her, shaking his head. He often seemed to be in some world of his own, as if he heard music we could not hear—or voices—or something.

That night he was sundered from us by more than mere distance as he walked back to us from Chicco; he was separated by more than his beauty. He was of a different species. His parents set him apart and were always with him; he was the sum of their history.

In his mind's eye, he once acknowledged, he saw them as if through the wrong end of binoculars; like tiny figures in a manger scene. Hirsch felt like a movie mogul as over and over, he'd restage the pogrom and supply it with a surprising ending. He would not have his parents run, but give in to the mob that had tasted Jew blood and gone crazy. He'd steel himself to it; he'd have them turn back to the mob, have them slaughtered like sheep, singing something holy. He'd linger on this scene, almost lovingly. The eerie stillness would settle in, the sound of never was, never to be. Hirsch smiled then; he shivered with an almost exquisite agony. They could have saved themselves so much disappointment, he thought; and they would have saved the world from him.

He wondered if there was a name for it. He asked Swinton one time if it was a disease. Swinton asked for the symptoms and Hirsch replied that he could not breathe; he was trapped in time, in that moment of pillage and murder and Jew blood in the streets. He lived it over and over, awake and asleep, as if he had been there and through it all himself. Somehow he was stuck in that moment and could not get beyond it.

Detaching himself from his horror, it was hard for Hirsch to remember who he was. But the act of atoning brought him to his senses again. That conquered everything.

If you told him you understood this or anything else about him, he got angry. "How can you?" he'd ask. "Did it happen to your folks?" He made a point of not being understood, for it would lessen his aloofness, violate his difference.

At the Alley, even with a crowd, he always seemed

alone, always thinking, unhappy, as he knew he should be.

We would get to know Hirsch after a time, after all those nights pitched away, one after another, like pennies in a toss game at the Alley. We liked him. His intensity threw us; yet he could be lighter-hearted when he was drinking. And there was his disturbing Jew beauty. It undercut everything, like only love or shadows do, with a violet rim of trembling. And, oh, we shivered in it nightly. Like his parents, Hirsch had not been with people much. He'd never speak of himself, the little things that filled his day. Dwin and Hilary had relaxed enough that first evening to rattle on nonstop about what woman bought what hat at Kerrison's; or in the men's department, whose huge foot was a not-to-be-believed—did it mean anything about the size of his you-know-what? Dwin wondered out loud—fourteen. Hirsch made us nervous with all the silence, taut as untouched harp strings.

But they _were_ touched, after all; they were touched and played upon by spectral hands that played tunes both horrific and terrifying. For Hirsch had not only a past; what was worse, he had a personality that he summed up primarily in the word that we had denied upon hearing, but in which he reveled. For us, it had come down from Swinton in the darkness; but for Hirsch, it was from heaven, spelled out in the Day of Atonement service. He confessed it was then that he first heard it, and the rabbi repeated it solemnly: _men shall not lay with men_ or some such thing, from a jealous deity; for this moon love the Lord would damn his infidel children.

Hirsch would never forget this, though sometimes it brought him close to violence. It was more real for him than for us; he kept it as a frontlet before his eyes; and like a daub of blood, marked his doorpost with it. It was his religion, that which determined him. If he could only spawn children, he could make sense of the past, could ease his parents' suffering; he could show them that their blood would go on. But he couldn't. He was doomed to the cold comfort to be extracted from other men's bodies.

So Hirsch had sidestepped love and completely bypassed pity. He would have nothing of consolation. When not beguiled, Hirsch would stare off into space, the stare becoming more and more intense with time, and with that his body tensing. It was mistaken for arrogance, and that became him. In the corner of his eye there seemed to be something he alone could see: a peasant woman screaming "They murdered my son!" *I wish they had murdered me*, he'd think. His muscles would tighten; he'd be drawing himself up into a knot; one time he clutched a glass so hard it shattered. Hirsch just ignored it and had Chicco bring him another drink. He looked at us all as if he wanted to kill somebody.

Which one would it be, he thought, as he looked us over and we looked back at him. Who would bear the Lord's vengeance and be punished with the pleasure of his body?

"Let it be me," each of us pleaded silently, that first night when we saw him in the Alley.

But more often than not, we saw, it was some old man who could damn Hirsch further by paying for it in specie.

After Hirsch had come back to sit with us, Chicco came over and they whispered together. The midget went away soon after with a smile on his face and his hands clasped behind his back. Then Hirsch himself rose. "Good night," he said, holding his chair up with one hand. "It's been a pleasure," he added ironically, as he put it back down.

I don't think he remembered a single name or thought of any of us as individuals.

He went up to the bar, where a balding man stood in the shadows. They left together almost immediately.

"I think that was Luden Renfrew." Dwin nudged me. I turned to get a closer look, but they had already disappeared.

"What do you suppose?" Hilary asked. He left the rest of the question unformulated, as if the answer would be too puzzling.

"Think," Dwin cried in rapture, in ecstasy. Those were poor Dwin's finest moments, when he could believe the worst about somebody. "Didn't you see Chicco bring him the money?"

The import of this sank in, and we were to see that it was only when there was no one else around to pay for it that Hirsch, needing release or damnation or maybe just being human after all and needing company, would look around the Alley for a likely candidate and then give it away for free.

Never in my wildest dreams did I think it would be me. I was too timid to even imagine it. I was too straitlaced and Hirsch was too handsome, too strange and exotic. He ignored me at work and barely acknowledged me in the Alley. But that look he had given us excited me. He stirred desires in me, and he also made me angry, for who did he think he was, a Jew to boot, to lord it over and ignore me? I hated it when I saw him leave with someone else. Just because he was good-looking was no cause to act the way he did. Flesh did not mean that much; or did it? I pondered this each evening after that, as I paced the oyster-shell walks at the Battery.

"*Is* it important?" that boy asked me last night.

"What do you think?" I asked back; he looked from his mirrored reflection back to me.

I'm sure we agreed.

bout this time, I began to go every night to the Battery. I'd stop by for a minute or two; I'd linger and hope; and every now and then I'd meet a stranger. One, I remember, took me back to his room in the St. John's Hotel. We had a drink. There was even some affection; and when it was done and I was leaving he turned to me and said, "Do you want any money?"

"No," I said.

"I'm not white," he told me.

"Huh!" I said; "what do you mean?" I held out my arm next to his; we were the same color. But the man—he was handsome—just shook his head.

"Only my father was," he said.

"I'm going now," I said.

He shrugged; "Go ahead; leaving ain't going to change anything." I looked back at his face. If I had stayed, I think he would have stopped right then; but his eyes were suddenly angry. He laughed like a madman. "I bet you never done it with a nigger before; how does it feel?"

I told myself it didn't matter, but I was horrified all the same, and half expected, as I ran down the corridor, that all those doors would open and people would pop out of them, wagging disapproving fingers at me. The next few nights I wondered which was worse: to be colored or queer? I was scared where these thoughts might lead, to what depths they might take me. I wouldn't go to the Battery for anything after that; but if Swinton said he was going, I joined him at the Alley.

We drank a lot down there and laughed even more. We even danced together on Fridays when there was music. Though we may have been damned, we were not daring, so we never danced the Charleston. We had some strong ideas against which there was no struggling. We made it home every night by eleven-thirty.

I was actually through the street door of my parents' house one night and reaching for the latchkey when I stopped. I listened. There was no sound; but I put the key back into the hiding place and went down the steps and across the silent streets to the Battery.

I felt called; every brick and leaf and slat of every shutter stood out in an utter moonlit clarity. I was excited, knowing that someone was waiting for me down at the park. I almost ran, wondering to whom it could be, this drive, this urge, this thing I called fate, was taking me.

It was cold down there when I arrived; there was a frozen moon and the wind whipping over the warmer water lifted up vapor; ghosts rose from the sea. I looked about but didn't see a soul; there was not a single car going by and no one sat on any of the benches that lined the streets. I was used to being fooled by desire, but I was still young enough to doubt that what I called my intuition could fail me. I was all for giving in to rotten bad luck when suddenly I saw a figure break from the dark park, distinguish itself from the tossing shadows, and walk across the street to the sea wall.

I left my bench, blew on my hands, and crossed his way. I ran through the few lines I had mastered for such occasions. I could ask that stranger what time it was . . . if he had the time; or if he was a tourist, where was he staying?

I approached, and the man held a match to his cigarette, held it a minute out of the wind so I could briefly see a face across which shadow and flame flowed. The match went out; the face disappeared. Then he turned out of the shadows of his high collar into the moonlight.

"Hirsch!"

I was surprised and so was he. I had seen him earlier that evening in the Alley, but he had left with Luden Renfrew some hours before; so what, I wondered, was he doing here? And what must he think of me? I was still Victorian enough to believe that no nice boy ever admitted to looking for sex. I fancied that it was something done in the dark, between beasts, kept in deepest secrecy, like a gentleman's charity. You didn't admit to it out here in front of God and everybody. I gasped at my blunder and mumbled something about not being able to sleep.

Hirsch, however, said nothing. He pulled on his cigarette, and looked across the water to James Island. I did not ask, but I did wonder; what had he done in those hours with Luden Renfrew? Were there other men there? Had he made a lot of money?

Hirsch kept his own counsel, finished his cigarette, and just stood looking at the light on the water, smiling enigmatically. "It's like a piano," he said softly.

Did Hirsch play? I wondered, watching the light linger on the tops of waves.

"None of your damn business," he said abruptly. "I didn't come here to chat," he said, as if it were the first time he'd really laid eyes on me.

"What did you come here for?" I asked in a second, amazed at my own bravery.

To be nonchalant, I tried not to look in his face. I knew I would be lost if I did.

Hirsch had not answered; he just shifted on his feet and I could not help myself. I looked, and was stabbed by his darkness, his size, but mostly by his luminous eyes; like an animal's in a trap, they were searching the dark. I was afraid of that need. I had to step back to fight his magnetic pull. It's good that he did what he did next, for I was unable to speak.

He took my hand and placed it on his crotch and began to stroke himself up and down with it. "That's why I'm here." His strong grip trapped my wrist and he seemed to enjoy the cruelty. We other boys had always conjectured as to what glories lay in Hirsch's pants; and had taken peeks in the WC.

"Wait till summer," Dwin had suggested. "Let's take him to the beach and I'll bet you'll see it peeking out of his trunks; it'll swing."

Hirsch moved my hand up and down. Through the fabric I could feel him stiffening. He let go of my hand and he smiled lightly. His lips parted and his eyes closed.

"Strong hands," he said, looking at me.

I laughed now. "My job, you know. I have to be . . ."

But his look silenced me. I coaxed the beast. I was getting excited when he suddenly broke away. "Hirsch, where are you going?" I called out.

He did not look back once; he calmly whistled and strode down the sea wall away from me. I looked around.

Down between two pools of yellow light sat an old ramshackle Ford. I ran toward it and reached it just as Hirsch slid in on the other side. He opened the opposite door for me.

"Yours?" I asked.

"Borrowed," he said.

I slammed the door and shivered, waiting for him to fire the ignition.

Instead, with one movement, he unbuttoned his trousers and pulled them down to his knees; he took them off.

"What are you doing?" I was aghast.

"Do you want it or not?" he sneered, looking down at his lap and back at me.

I looked at him and he knew; "In the car?"

"You got some better place?"

"No."

He propped his back against the door, one arm over the

cracked leather seat, the other over the steering wheel, one leg on the floorboard, the other straddling the seat; he sat there as his cock rent the atmosphere.

"Do you need an invitation? Or what?"

I looked all around to make sure; and when I was bending down gingerly toward it, his hands became a crown on my head and he impaled me. His pelvis thrust. I stuck my face into his crotch and obliterated my mouth like a kid in a watermelon-eating contest. He ground his body into my lips; his excitement doubled mine. Even when he hit the horn and jerked up to see if anyone had heard, I could not release him.

Hirsch sucked on his lips and ran one hand down his swelling chest, and I bent before him. He was mumbling. We went at it for hours it seemed, until our satisfactions came, pulled from us with anguish, with grief, as if we were tortured and unwilling. Hirsch was transcended to some place beyond speech.

I lay collapsed against the seat, trying to gather up the scattered bits of me; and then he came back. I could see it in his eyes, narrowing, focusing.

With no pity, he took my face in his hands and looked into my eyes; then he pushed me away. I thought he would spit. His lips bunched in disdain and contempt, as if he were disgusted. "You ready," he said.

With no further warning, he lifted me up and bent me over the back seat. "What are you doing?" It reminded me of the way my father would bend me over and drop my drawers for speaking disrespectfully. He tugged my pants down. Then he spit on his palms. And I could feel him rubbing up against me.

I thought boys could only do one thing; and this union seemed to be taboo; it seemed to be the ultimate perversity, this madman's aping of normality.

"Hirsch!" I nearly screamed.

It was my first time—and the feeling of an alien immensity moving in your body! He was pitiless. He held me around my waist and got me.

I thought he would never finish but he suddenly shivered as if he had been struck; he bucked wildly and then froze. Then he collapsed on my back and lay his sweaty head on my shoulder almost gently.

Something wet hit my face; I was too aware of my own tears then to realize that he, too, had been crying.

In a while he drew away and fell back down behind the wheel. He reached for his pants.

"Where do you live?" he asked a little later, combing his hair in the mirror. It was the first thing he said to me.

I did not answer but he already knew and drove me there.

"I'll see you around," he said.

I tried leaving the car without looking at him. But he grabbed me by the wrist and twisted it back. I tried to wriggle free but his grasp grew tighter. "Say good night," he said.

"Good night."

He laughed, released me, and drove off.

I ran from the car and hardly made it upstairs before I got sick. What pleasure there had been had transcended into pain. I washed and washed and slept feverishly. I felt tainted with him, as if he had invaded my soul. I scrubbed and scrubbed but his smell was still on me. I spent that next day in bed, disgusted with myself and revolted by Hirsch. I'd never let him do that again, I vowed. It was against nature. I wouldn't; I was from a good Savannah family. And I played that part the next few days, being affectionate to my elders, being well-dressed in the streets. I held aloof from the trashy boys at the Peacock Alley.

But I discovered Hirsch liked that. He watched me from a distance with approval in his eyes. There was more to it than that, however: like a dog, he had found out my secret, snuffed out the scent of disgust and fear. He had me treed. He'd bow and tip a nonexistent hat at me when he went by. He'd smile sardonically. I ignored him; and after a couple of nights of peace, he approached me in the Alley.

"I'll give you a ride home," he said by way of a greeting.

"No, thank you," I replied icily. "I'm staying here."

He smiled. "Not for long. I'll go get us a drink."

"Fool!" Dwin hissed in my ear. "What's wrong with you?" He looked at me in disbelief.

Even Hilary, usually as placid as a cow, noticed something.

"Why didn't you say yes?" Swinton wanted to know.

"I don't know," I replied.

"Who does?"

I made a face.

"Try me."

I did try, but words, I discovered, were useless, as heavy as rocks in my mouth; they could only confound me. I was not adroit enough, nor had I been indoctrinated. Only later would I realize that Hirsch had made it my fault. I was to blame that he was queer.

Hirsch came back our way and his shadow fell across the table. A hush fell too; we stopped speaking. He had two drinks in his hand; and he reached out and handed one to me. I ignored it.

Then he put it down on the table and moved it in my direction.

"Drink," he said.

I continued speaking to Hilary, who fell back silenced in his seat.

Hirsch said my name sternly.

I looked up at him and then back down; I could feel his gaze, like a physical weight, pressing down on me; and then there was his beauty. I tried to throw them off; it was his will against mine. Nothing had ever been so important in all my life till then. I held my breath, concentrating.

"Drink it, dammit."

I zeroed in on the glass, trying to make the rest of the world disappear.

It was the force of his voice that scared me. And it was the gaze I felt—not just his; everyone there was looking at me. I was ashamed.

Hirsch glared above me, as if he were punishing a dog that would not heel.

I held off as long as I could. My temples started to throb

and I knew my face was red. I felt like I was suffocating.

In a rush, I gave in. I could feel myself relaxing, melting. A sound bounced back at me oddly. I collapsed, and it wasn't so bad after all. It was like the giving in that a drowning man must feel. Like some psychic tide, I could feel Hirsch's victory flowing into me. My arm rose up to the drink. I was giddy and I gave in and took it, and the others he supplied, too. He must have changed his mind about leaving. Every few minutes he would come back to check on me, getting me ready, I suppose. He did not even deign to speak.

"Come on," he finally said, crooking his finger. And I stood, forgetting the sensations I had had the other night, but remembering that first look he had given me. I followed him out of the Peacock Alley. I walked past Dwin, past Hilary and Swinton, all of them turning their eyes on me. I could actually feel their assembled envy.

Once outside, Hirsch led me down one of those graveled and glass-strewn alleys between the buildings.

Looking around, I could see a blanket on the ground; blank walls rose up in every direction; and the moon crept up over the parapets to look down on us.

Hirsch disrobed; so did I. But not all the way. He only took off what he had to, and then he reached out for me. I thought of gladiators preparing.

There were no preludes; like a wrestler he reached out and we went right to it. We made sounds like alley cats did, backing up to one another. Hirsch was frenzied. And he seemed to be blaming me for this aberration that had come over him. When Hirsch was done he got up, brushed himself off, dressed. I looked up at him and he nodded back down at me. It was only after he left that I got up too. I went home without thinking of anything; and the next night I returned to the Alley. And the next night too. We had silently made a treaty. I had stepped out of the clarity of winter into a hazed and humid summer atmosphere. My perceptions were like the air was then—blurred, dream-edged, fuzzed, and murky. I cannot say that I went against my will those next few weeks.

All I can recall is that when he was ready he would come for me.

He had no shame. Oh no, he delighted in flaunting his claim over me. He'd blow the horn of his borrowed car in front of my parents' house; he'd stop me at work; he'd come up to collect me in the Alley. "Come on," he'd say, and I'd go.

From a depth, from a distance, I could see myself and wonder dimly if it was love or just a lust that was so strong it seemed like destiny. When he was there I did not need to think. And when he was gone, I rubbed myself, remembering.

There is this memory: I am looking up at him; Hirsch and the pockmarked moon are staring down at me. As we couple, his head eclipses the moon. It is darkness and light, darkness and light. He is light, plumbing the darkness of me. For me it was life, but Hirsch was angry. He was punishing me for triggering such responses in him, revealing such a vulnerability.

I did not exist without Hirsch. I needed his smell to revive me, his breath to resuscitate me, his imprint, his fingermarks, to remold me. I needed him to rouse me from my trance, and when I was dismissed and he let me go, I slipped back into a half-dreaming state that was a reverie of him.

I saw him at work, passed him in the hall; like an unseen ghost, I prayed for him to conjure me.

I became as insatiable as he was; but I wanted even more. I wanted him to use words, too: one in particular. It would be like the last rites if he said "love" over me.

But Hirsch hardly spoke.

"See you tomorrow," was all he'd give me when we were done; and though I swore, no, I will not go, I ended up there just the same.

No self-respect at all, I'd arrive first at that colored "rooming house" on Berresford Street. We had looked for a whorehouse for our meetings. The signal in those days was not a red light, but a rather tiny mattress, the size of a crib's, hung over the banister of an upstairs porch.

We met and entered through an archway into a fouled

court overhung by a sweeping tree that was an intense green even in winter. The similarity of the layout with that of the Confederate Home later made me think of Chinese boxes— how one could have fit inside the other—later I saw how one event was contained in another; and how it has come down all these years.

The ramshackle stairs bucked beneath our feet as we ran; there were rotted-out holes in the piazza floors and clumsily patched railings. A series of cell-like rooms opened up from the porch, each having a bed and a washstand; there were no windows per se, but in the back wall was a small rectangular opening with no glass, just a rusted, latticed grate that allowed in air and offered a vine-obstructed view of the jungle that lay behind the building. Some of the rooms reeked of urine. From others you could peer out and see amorphous statuary in the overgrown garden of a deserted house.

We'd go along the upstairs gallery, silently as monks. Once the door was latched, Hirsch would take hold of me. Springs—if we had a bed with them (sometimes the mattress was just corn husks on wood slattings)—would groan and squeak. Hirsch tried to get through me as if I were a doorway to another sphere.

If we tarried longer than the hour that our money allowed, the proprietor, a big colored man, would bang on the door and shout, "Hey, don't you mens make a home in there."

So Hirsch would have to get out of bed and wrap that dismal shroudlike sheet around him and come round to me. I'd dig into my pockets for a quarter and hand it to him, and then Hirsch would go to the door, open it an inch, and hand it out. We'd hear the man shuffling away, whistling a song that never changed in rhythm, tune, or melancholy. Then Hirsch would turn back.

"Haven't had enough, huh?"

I'd drop to my knees.

It was on one of those short winter afternoons after one of our bouts that I fell asleep and did not wake until it was almost dark. A lilac-colored twilight was the medium in

which the world lay suspended; there was a sweet languor to
my bones; not really awake, still half asleep, I felt like a
plum, perhaps; juicy and hanging off the tree, ripe almost to
bursting. Plum-colored, too, were the shapes of Hirsch's
hands, the bruises I saw blooming on my body.

There was a sound like a gunshot. I started, and though
I was not asleep I felt nevertheless a sense of awakening. I
had to blink, not just in the light, but in the presence of a
thought that had appeared, full blown, like a Venus.

I got up and went to the window to follow the sound;
and in the garden behind us I could see a lichen-eaten statue
that had no face, no arms, nothing. A haunted thing, it
taunted itself with what it used to be. I turned back to look
at Hirsch lying in bed. He was still facedown asleep.

Everything in the room seemed changed now; the
stained walls, grimed by time, their many colors iridescent
like a dragonfly's wings, disappearing into the rising tide of
evening. Time, I saw, had conquered and mellowed; plaster
had cracked; passion had been spent and a fine powder of
mortar (or mortality?) sifted down from the ceiling. I felt as
if I had ash in my mouth. That nasty thing in the garden had
so worried me that I searched for my clothes and quickly put
them back on. I slipped out, leaving Hirsch asleep.

I found Swinton in the Medical College library. His
eyes, I saw, were ringed with fatigue, but I did not hesitate.
(None of us knew it then, not even he, that the disease that
would dismember him was beginning.) Swinton looked up
from his work. He sighed, put down his pencil, and asked,
"What is it?"

"Nothing," I answered; "Can we get out of here?"

We went outside and stood under the magnolias. With
their leaves rustling coldly, I tried to tell him how Hirsch
seemed driven to find some evil deep inside me. Find it and
root it out with an almost evangelical fury. "Swinton," I
said, "he scares me."

Swinton sighed. "But don't you like him?" We turned
back toward the building.

"I do," I said.

"And does he like you?"

"How should I know?"

"Has he said anything to you?"

"No; nothing at all; and that's just it, Swinton. He won't tell me a damn thing. He won't say a word. I think he's scared to. I think he's scared of me; he's scared of you, too, and Dwin, and Hilary. Of anything that's not him. It's all a threat. I don't know what I mean," I said, breaking off. In the dark and cold I felt lost and helpless, but worse: I knew Hirsch would come here and find me and take me back to that room on Berresford Street and make me crazy.

I was so tense I caught myself opening and closing my fist. "Jesus, look at me! I've never done this before. He's making me like him, Swinton!"

"But doesn't love do that?" Swinton asked. He had been in love once but he shared the details of it with no one. "What do you want to do now?"

"Let's leave."

So Swinton went in to get his books and I sat out in the dark, realizing that I was a portal of sorts for Hirsch. For I was his sin; and through me, I realized, he sought deliverance.

I told Swinton that when he came back out.

"And do you think he will find it?" he asked

"I don't know."

We went over to his house and stayed up talking. But around 4:00 A.M. he said I had to go. He said he was tired, and maybe he should step down as president of the Sons of Wisteria Society.

ut it was I who took sick the next day, not Swinton, and that was not surprising. For what better thing was there for me to do than abdicate, leave the field, wave the white flag, and give up entirely? I took to my bed and I did not get out of it that next morning. And I am sure it was only my inability to believe in myself that saved me, those next few weeks, from working myself up into an in-

curable disease. My chills and fever were real enough, but
there was nothing really wrong with me, other than youth
and pride and fear—none fatal in themselves. In my fevered
dreams, I'd think I was Hirsch, but then I'd wake up realizing
I was only me. And Hirsch was a toxin going through me.
My head was clearing. But my heart festered.

Hilary brought me a book to read; Dwin kept me in
gossip; but Swinton just sat with me. He could comfort with
his mere presence, without saying a thing. I do not think he
believed at all in the science of healing. To him it was a
special mystical thing. He worked his wonders on me. One
day he'd come in bearing fruit; the next day, chocolate; and
once, out of the blue, he walked in and put his hands over
my eyes. "Guess who's here?" he demanded.

I would not play along.

"Someone who likes you a lot."

I pulled away from him to check myself in the mirror.
"You don't mean?"

"Yes, I do! Ta da!" Swinton called out. I fell backward
as Ned Grimke walked in. He advanced and kept his eyes
down as shyly as a child bride being led up to the altar. He
stuck out something wrapped in tissue. But I would not take
it.

Maybe it was the sudden movement, but my head
reeled.

"It's for you," Ned said, holding it out.

"Thanks very much," I said.

"Open it!"

In the tissue there were some benne seed wafers.

"My aunts made them," he said. "I asked them to." He
smiled at me.

It's good that social graces include many forms of lying.
"They're fine," I told him as I nibbled one. I put the box
down; I hated benne seed.

I spoke to Swinton through clenched teeth. "You
should have told me you were bringing someone. I could
have arranged some tea."

"Your mother saw us," he said, sitting down gratefully.
"She told us to tell you some's on the way up."

"Sorry to hear you're sick," Ned said. He sat down on the edge of the bed, but jumped up when I warned him to keep his distance. I told him he might catch something from me. I didn't like the way his eyes lingered on my face; I reached for the book on the bedstand.

"What are you reading?"

I held up the book and Ned moved his lips.

Swinton read it for him. Ned was about to say something to me, but Swinton interrupted. "Ned's eyes are funny," he said. "I don't understand it; no one does; but he gets things confused, reverses and even upside-downs things." Then he poked around in his pocket for a piece of paper and a nub of a pencil. "Go on, Ned," he said, extending them to him.

Ned took the sheet and handed it back to me when he was done.

It looked like code.

"Thanks," I said, handing it back. "Is that a new language ya'll have concocted?"

Swinton took it from Ned and motioned for me to wait; then, like an impresario, he held it to the small mirror on the table near my bed. The letters, undecipherable at first, now spelled *Grimke*.

It reminded me of what my Dah had told me once; that if you read the Scriptures backward and had evil in your soul, you could conjure the devil to appear.

We did not say anything for a while. My mother knocked and came in, bringing in a tray of tea.

So we spoke of other things under her auspices—who was seeing whom, how Swinton needed to rest, and just when was he going to set a good example for us younger boys and settle down and get married? Swinton, ever the gentleman, said that she was the only one for him, and he had to make excuses, pretending to visit me to see her. My mother and he flirted with each other shamelessly.

I had been too shy to bring it up with Hilary or Edwin; but when my mother left the room, I asked Swinton if he had seen Hirsch or if he had said anything about me.

"I've seen him," he said, "but he's not said a thing." He looked solemnly, directly, into my eyes.

"You're sure?"

He nodded. Sometimes I wished Swinton was the sort to make things up instead of always speaking the truth. He tried his best to cushion it. "Hirsch has been acting so oddly," he said; "he's so out of control. He laughs so loudly."

"Wonderful," I said, sinking back on the pillows.

"But don't misunderstand," Swinton was quick to jump in. "It sounds like he's crying. I don't know what's up with him, but he's going to explode one day if he keeps it up."

"You're *sure* he's never asked about me?"

"Not once; he's made a point of it."

"But don't you think that means something?"

"It must," he agreed.

I wondered then if it meant that Hirsch was mad; it could have been that he was angry at my desertion but was too proud to allow me the satisfaction of knowing I could hurt him. "Swinton, do you think it means he's starting to care for me?"

"I wonder," he said.

Just then, Ned reached for something. He was in the far corner of the room with a glass paperweight in his hand through which he was looking at the light. I had forgotten about him. I was mad at Swinton for bringing him here, and mad at Ned for not being Hirsch. "Do you know Hirsch?" I asked Ned. I could tell he had been listening.

"No," he said, turning back to look at me. "I'm sorry."

"Well, no need to be," Swinton said. "We'll all get together one night and take you to the bar we go to."

"Swinton," I warned; but before I could stop him, he had forged on. "We go to a bar on French Ending Street; it's called the Peacock Alley."

We both stared at him to see his reaction, but it seemed to mean nothing to Ned. It nevertheless worried me; I did not want him to know I was a moon lover or anything else about me.

"I'd like to go with ya'll," Ned said. Forgetting Swinton, he focused all his attention, funneled all his intensity on me. "That would be fun. It would be good to be friends again, like we were when we were kids." He shot a quick look at me, but turned away when I did.

"What are you doing in town?" I asked him.

"Looking for a job," he said.

"Cousin Ned's an artist," Swinton put in.

"Oh, no I'm not!" Ned colored and looked at Swinton. "Not really." He was looking at Swinton now with a pleading in his face, as if to say, "You promised not to tell anybody."

"You're too modest." Swinton turned to him. "Beat your own drum, Ned, or no one else will. You should see his things."

"I have a studio in the Confederate Home," Ned said apologetically.

"What do you do there?"

Ned looked at his palms, obviously not wanting to talk about it, but I persisted.

At first he was embarrassed, as if it was something unusual, a secret pleasure, to talk about himself. It could have been because of being so lonely. As he talked on, I noticed that this was the first time since we were small that I saw some sort of animation come over him. It was like a wax mask suddenly taking on expression.

"They're not anything," he said, trying to describe his drawings. "I just practice; I do designs and colors and things." His eyes shifted to the bed table. I had wrapped his package back up in tissue and put it on the tray with all the empty tea things. Ned looked at it. "Don't you like them?" he asked.

"I do!" I answered. "But they should just be put in the ice box."

Ned just stared at the package.

"I would like to go with both of you to the bar," he repeated woodenly; "but I have to go now." He came over and shook my hand. He shook hands with Swinton, too. "My aunts are expecting me."

"I'll see you on Tuesday at Miss Wragg's," Swinton

called out as Ned left. And when he was gone, he turned to me. "What do you think?"

I said nothing for a while and then confessed, "I don't trust him."

"Why not?" He looked surprised.

"He's hiding something."

"He's just shy."

"He's evil."

Swinton was incredulous. "Come on! Do you have a temperature?" He came over and put his hand on my forehead.

"You *are* feverish," Swinton said, "and imagining things."

"No I'm not," I said, brushing him off. "It's just you, Swinton. You won't think bad about anybody."

"Well, I'm sure he's got a lot of talent," Swinton said. "You should see his studio—he's a sculptor, too—it's pretty amazing. It's like he's got all the ideas right, but just needs a spark to set him going." Swinton went on, talking a blue streak, but I wasn't listening. I knew what I wanted; I could feel my desire stir and rise under the sheets, and was ashamed that Swinton might see it too. For the first time in the weeks since I had gotten ill, I wanted to be somewhere else besides my bed. I wanted to rush out and find Hirsch in the Alley.

"Where do you think you're going?" Swinton asked, when I tried to. "You get right back in there. You tell me if you need anything."

I needed Hirsch. (What could I say?) Seeing the hunger in Ned's eyes had triggered it. He set me on edge; he depressed me.

When Swinton left, I vowed I would get well. I would get out of bed soon and I'd find Hirsch Hess. I'd find him and ask him to forgive me.

I was up and around a few days later, but it was already too late. Maybe there was no malice aforethought; maybe there was no conspiracy; maybe it was just one of those things. Whatever it was, it was at Miss Wragg's that I missed my chance to make amends with Hirsch.

It must have been a Tuesday, for that was the night she kept for entertaining. To us, it was like stepping into history, going down the walkway to her door off Chalmers Street, or trying, as we had as kids on the beach, to match our strides to those bigger folk who had preceded us there. All sorts of famous people visited Miss Wragg; every poet, prince, prima ballerina, or dignitary to visit Charleston was taken here. One of her most loyal devotees, or her "boys," as she called her followers, was Saint Julian Wentworth, the most famous poet of the city. He had her alone on Mondays; we considered ourselves fortunate to have her at all, even in company; for it was exciting to go there, a different atmosphere. One never knew what she would speak of next in her front room—her neighbor Josephine's garden party, Freud, or the mating rites of Pygmies. And "I have nothing at all against homosexuals," she said one evening, in her precise voice, to the sudden chill of we boys who sat at her feet pretending *it doesn't apply to me,* "except that no one I know who is that way is happy."

I wonder if that may tend to explain two things: why she never married, as well as the gender of those who turned up on Tuesday; mostly we who came were men, the hopeful, the published and the not, the dreamers, the believers; it was as if Miss Wragg was our witch doctor and her wisdom our fetish. She was avoided like the plague by the ladies. And it had nothing to do with snobbery or the fact that she was a Massachusetts Yankee. I think that it had to do with the fact that they felt her judging them. (Or it could have been that they suspected Miss Wragg—as I did myself sometimes—of being a secret member of the Daughters of Sappho Society.) "It's just that she's so cold," the ladies would say, making their excuses. (As cold as a marble goddess, as lovely.) Perhaps they were jealous of the Ulmann photographs they saw of her, posed in profile—in three-quarter, in front of a frieze of three Greek deities—Miss Wragg: tall, straight, statuesque and hollow-cheeked. When you met or parted she stood and took your hand; she refused even kisses on the cheek, avoided anything that vaguely hinted of sentimentality. It was her cold blue eyes, how they appraised things, that gained her so many enemies. Miss Wragg had the first scientific mind in Charleston. She judged things with an acuteness of mind that was as sharp as her gaze, as cutting. Though of the most faultless bloodlines, of a genealogy that even the St. Cecilia could approve, she had always been democratic; hers was the only salon in Charleston where your merit and not your birth gained you entry. You just knocked and were admitted without ceremony.

Today, however, I hear things have deteriorated sadly. Last night a boy told me that it is like threading your way through a maze to get to her now, as difficult as reaching the Oracle at Delphi. First, I hear, you must arrange to meet a friend of hers who has a key. Then he'll lead you through the gate, down the dank and vine-hung walkway, through the door and up the many steep and narrow steps. You are told to sit in the front room while the guide goes across the hall to see if omens augur well, if Miss Wragg is awake or in the mood for company. You cannot help but admire the walls, peacock blue, hung with dolls from Japan, medieval ivories, and bits and pieces left not just by the Cooper and the Ashley, but by the others of civilization—the Nile, the Amazon, the Ganges. Those who have come there hear the tap-tap-tap of her cane; as with a drum roll and a trumpet, ta-da-ta-da, she is announced. Miss Wragg is coming.

Gaunt and stooped with white hair, a grotesque harpy, she appears on the arm of her friend, and smiles. She must be nearly ninety. You are instantly pressed into her service. You bow and scrape and help to fold up old knees. It is a job getting her down into that chair and her feet up on the ottoman.

It is done; and you say hello.

Fool! Didn't you know Miss Wragg is deaf; that for twenty years she has heard nothing?

"You have to write it down," you are told by her friend. He hands you a pad and a pencil and stands behind her chair with his arms crossed, like a protecting genie.

Once you have written, she takes the pad into her gnarled hand and tilts it to the light, as if she were a seer and these were entrails she is consulting; her eyes through her bubble lenses are large, pale blue, and frightening. She pats the cat, black (named Guido), smiles, and speaks.

"So good to see you, too."

After a while, the interpreter steers the "conversation" to what the boys want to hear. Sometimes she will not cooperate and they have to return; Miss Wragg will take their faces in her hands, reading their features with her eighty-odd-year-old eyes and fingers.

If you tell her you've come to hear about Hirsch and Ned, she'll clasp your face in her hands and stroke your hair. "Aaahh . . ." she says, in her deaf woman's voice, measuring it out like an old actress, emphasis for emphasis. But watch those eyes, wild behind the lenses, like a vampire's, blood hungry.

If she were that, a crucifix and a Bible would be of use to you. But she is Miss Wragg. You need only the Bible; need only to open it to the part where it reads (and repeat it over and over to yourself as she speaks), "All is vanity."

For, "Yes, it was I," she will tell you proudly. "I brought them together." She will pause, and will sometimes, I am told, forget what she is saying, and tip the glass of white liqueur that burns like fire, and say, by way of nothing, "I introduced Strega—it is Greek for witch—to Charles Towne." Oh, she is careful to smile, and to pronounce the eighteenth-century spelling as if she were responsible for founding the whole town, instead of only one of its phenomena. She'll swallow and return to what she has been saying.

"It was one of those cool and crisp and utterly still evenings when Hirsch and Ned met. It was winter. We had been looking through Maspero that week, studying the cult of Isis, I believe. There was a knock at the door. . . ." Here she pauses; she remembers so intently that even her listeners sense the years retreating. They look up at the doorway to see if Hirsch is there; they glance at her feet to Ned Grimke; but they are gone. She sighs, and is a withered thing that once was lovely.

✳

She was that night. I remember her as being particularly stunning in her gray silk; but then everything in the world seemed so new and clear to me. It was my first time out of bed in nearly two weeks.

When I arrived there was a fire in the coal grate and Miss Wragg sat in her armchair in the corner; on the wall above her hung the frieze of the three Greek deities. Plates lay upon the table with traces of the crème de menthe she had poured over cake and ice cream. The Masperos were open. Hilary sat politely with his hands crossed over his knees on the white, elephant-eared settee, Swinton was on a hassock, and Dwin on top of the bookshelf that doubled as a window seat. Ned had come with Swinton, his first time here, and sat with his hands clasped around his knees, at Miss Wragg's feet. He looked up happily and nodded at me. All over the walls were masks, relics from dead civilizations, souvenirs from countless cultures and numerous epochs, the stranded debris of centuries.

Miss Wragg glanced up then; when our eyes met she smiled, and without missing a beat, she turned back to the long loose sheets of printing in her lap. I sat on the rug and tucked up my knees.

"Swinton," I said, "what is it?"

But he said nothing. I thought he was removed from the world, enraptured by what he heard. (But he wasn't; he had been to the doctor that day and had found out the cause of his killing fatigue.) Swinton looked up at me blankly.

"Shh," Dwin said, admonishing me with a finger on his lips. "It's the poet's new book."

I saw the red pencil in Miss Wragg's hand; she added punctuation and corrected spelling as she read through the galleys out loud. If Saint Wentworth had gotten delirious and rhapsodized over some romantic-sounding impossibility, it was Miss Wragg who set him straight, making sure the right bird sang the correct note, and annotating his margins to prevent any other errors in natural history.

I can still remember the sound of her voice: matter-of-fact, but capable of subtle shades of feeling. She read poem after poem, letting the sheets unfurl about her feet. The absent writer's images materialized slowly—buzzards in stark trees, marsh-sunk sunsets, and new moons rising unseen from the sea. Essences, miasmas of the low country. Their sounds showered down like sparks from an anvil. And then there was a poem about Charleston herself, dusk settling about, the poet pulling it around him like a shawl. I remember the thrill; she read of St. Michael's chimes as, across the cold street, the bells rang nine-fifteen; someone was knocking.

It usually was Swinton who took it upon himself to let in the late entries.

I looked at him. His prematurely graying hair seemed grayer, his face the color of the ash that dangled from his burnt-out cigarette. Sitting tailor fashion, he rocked back and forth.

His eyes, always so fetching against his dark hair and skin, now had a sheen. I had never seen him so moved. The knocking continued. Hilary had dozed off. So I volunteered.

It was cold in the hall. In front of the Palladian window on the stairs there was a bust of Rousseau. White. Ghostly. Shaking myself from the trance of poetry, I opened the door.

The cold rushed in like water and I saw those dark wild eyes: they bore right through me.

"Hirsch!"

My heart beat wildly; for this was the first time I had seen him since I took sick.

I called his name again, my hand to my throat; "It sure is good to see you."

He said nothing.

I had been afraid before—of what I might do, of what I might give up—for him. Everything; and now I realized it was just that which had frightened me. I had a great respect for myself (I was young), but still I knew I would have thrown it all away for Hirsch. I wanted him. It was stronger than the fear. But Hirsch just stood there, glaring at me.

Not for a second did I think of her. Though Miss Wragg knew we were moon lovers, and spoke of sex, she herself did not seem to need the stimuli of bodies; and so those in her house were expected to act likewise.

Hirsch's cheeks were freezing and his arms immobile as I rubbed my hands up and down him; I pressed against his chest. "I'm so glad to see you." I put my hand against his crotch. "Let's leave."

But Hirsch was sullen and seemed angry. He pulled back and made a face as if disgusted.

"What's the matter?" I asked, closing the door. He leaned against the wall to catch his breath. Then, as I moved forward, he moved back. It was as if I were an assassin. He looked warily at me.

"What is it, Hirsch?" I asked him where he had been.

"Nowhere," he deigned to answer.

"Oh, come on," I demanded; but now I believe it; for he *could* disappear into his own world, beyond time or territory. Sometimes, sitting with his parents after supper, he could hear a baby crying. He'd see his mother's hands twitch and clasp and then she'd hold her fingers twisted in front of him, crying, "Hirsch, they ache; they want to hold grandchildren." Then he'd realize that she was washing the dishes and he had been hallucinating.

"You can tell me."

But he didn't. I suppose there had not been a soul around, except Chicco, at the Alley. No strangers wandered the streets and not a single car patrolled the Battery. So I suppose he had come to Miss Wragg's, remembering it was a Tuesday. Maybe, I thought excitedly, he had come in hopes of finding me.

"I'm glad you made it," I said; "wherever it was you were. I've missed you. Really." He looked surprised. It tumbled out. "I had time to think while I was sick. You could have come to visit me. I love you, Hirsch. I do; truly."

"You what?" He looked at me as if I were mad. "You don't even know me." He said it as though he was boasting.

And I guess he was, proud that he had remained aloof and inviolate and kept his dignity. "Hirsch, I'd like to get to know you," I said, flustered. "Let me. You're too hard on yourself, I think." Then I was coy, I ruffled his collar or something. He stiffened at my touch.

I had done it now, I realized. And there was no chance of undoing it. He was so angry with me I thought he might hit me. But then I saw understanding move his brow and a smile break over his face, lighting up his eyes with cruelty. He relaxed. I wanted to reach out and draw back that minute; but he was already growing distant. I had violated his privacy and this was not allowed. Boys could have his body; even old men and midgets could, for money, but his soul was his own.

"Get your hands off me," he said in an even tone, showing no emotion. I could have taken anger, but it was that lack of emotion that chilled me. The pleasure he got denying himself to me! I saw all at once that he would make me suffer, just as he had suffered. If I had frustrated his need for relief, then he'd return the favor. Tit for tat. But he'd repay me tenfold. He started up the stairs.

"Hirsch, please."

He turned back slowly.

"Remember how it was?" I told him I would pay for the room. All music to his ears, no doubt. Hirsch hung there at the foot of the stairs. He smiled, savoring his perverse pleasure. Why did he not speak?

Because he was Hirsch, a Jew: he had assumed the burdens carried by all the sons of Solomon; he was the sinned against and the sin, all the hideous conundrums.

One by one, smiling as he climbed, he mounted the steps deliberately, each step a blow.

I'll never forget the face that looked down on me that last time. And I swear, though I was raised in a town of unexplained sounds and mysterious happenings, and though my Dah had filled my head with haints, voodoo, and the evil of the moon, still I never believed in ghosts until that moment. There was Hirsch's sudden change to convince me.

He seemed possessed of some demon energy. You could almost feel it coming off him, in waves, like a heat.

I suppose that there were no demons, though Dah would have argued differently. Hirsch was just full of himself; he believed in himself more than anyone I have ever known.

I ran up the stairs after him; I passed Rousseau and as I reached the top, he stopped in the doorway to the drawing room. I would have pleaded with him, but the door to the front room was open; I could hear Miss Wragg reading. They would have been able to hear me.

The back of his head eclipsed my view of the room. Light came out in a broad ray, but he split it, like Moses and the Red Sea. Dwin, sitting in front of Ned, was first to see. He pointed in horror, but then screamed "Oh my God."

Angrily, Miss Wragg looked up.

At her feet, with his eyes rolled up and around in their sockets, his pasty face damp and green-hued, drawn up like a puppet, was Ned. At first I had thought he was going to say something; at first he had looked happy, beatific. He had looked at Hirsch; he had smiled at him. He had reached out; it was obvious he was trying to say something, but he could not speak. Hirsch stared at him. Ned's eyes filled with light and then clouded. For a moment he wavered, like a feather caught between two air drafts, suspended, not yet falling. Hirsch entered the room like a conqueror; I stayed back in the hallway. Behind him I could see what was happening. I saw his fists release. Hirsch seemed to let go of something.

There was still that half second when anything could have happened. Hirsch could have relented. Ned could have caught himself. Miss Wragg could have gone on reading. But then the interval was over. Hirsch willed it; he set his sights on that new boy at Miss Wragg's feet. He let his beauty loose on him. That was the beginning of it all.

The moment was over and Ned careened.

He kicked and convulsed and his whole torso shook; his eyes were up again and his arms jerked as if shocked. He writhed on the floor like a snake. You could hear the dreadful gurgle and gasp as he almost swallowed his tongue.

It was horrible. Ned gasped for air. Hilary came over to help; he leaned over Ned, but hopped away with a yelp when Ned kicked him in the knee.

Ned rolled and plunged; and Hilary looked up apologetically, as if it were his fault.

"Oh, make him stop, Miss Wragg; make him stop." Dwin clasped his hands together and shivered in what seemed to be sympathy, but which wasn't of course. "Miss Wragg," he called again.

All our eyes had turned instinctively to her. But she was still frozen in the moment; anything could happen to Miss Wragg still. She had dealt with stubbornness, suspicion, and outright bigotry; she had moved the hulking Ramses; nothing before in Charleston had been too big for her. This time, however, she knew she was up against something greater. Only she saw it, while we, who fancied ourselves so grown up, were oblivious. Looking back, I realize we were so untouched by experience, we were nearly as featureless as dumplings. We thought it was epilepsy. Only she realized what was happening, and it frightened her.

She turned to Swinton.

"You're an intern," she said, grabbing him. "Do something."

All our eyes were on him next; and that was awful, too; with the way Swinton now looked, it seemed as though the contagion were spreading. Swinton stared in disbelief at Ned and then back at Miss Wragg. He was like a stutterer in mid-syllable, poised in that suspenseful half moment.

"For God's sake, help him."

Ned backed up violently against the harp-legged table, overturning it. The sound brought Miss Wragg back to the world of flesh and stone and epilepsy.

"Get me a spoon," she demanded. And in the pandemonium, in the tilting lamplight, someone dashed by. I fell into a cane-bottomed seat.

That terrible gurgling sound in the back of Ned's throat made me think of Hirsch's cock; the way I'd gagged on it. Remembering, I chewed on my hand and nearly broke through the chair. I bit myself till there was blood in my mouth. I had to do something.

A shadow flashed through from the kitchen. Swinton broke out of his daze, righted the lamp, and the world turned from slanting light and dark to a pattern of geometric regularity. He tried to help Miss Wragg with Ned, but, having failed her once, she would have nothing more to do with him.

"That's quite all right," she said, brushing him aside.

"Miss Wragg, you don't understand."

I hated to see Swinton plead.

"You don't understand, Miss Wragg. I went to the doctor yesterday . . ."

She did not listen. She went down on her knees and dove for Ned. She grabbed his chin with one hand and with the other she stuck the spoon in his mouth. Her smile was grim.

And when his tongue ceased to flail, she clasped her fingers around his wrists. He fought her; but she overcame him. She deliberately regulated her own breathing as if it would encourage him. The spasms grew weaker and weaker.

"There, there," she said. She slipped to the floor and lifted his head to her lap.

Hilary came up and loosened his collar. Miss Wragg pushed him away.

Slowly, regularly, like flood water receding, Ned's breathing fell back into a more natural rhythm. She looked up victoriously for a second and stroked his damp golden hair with a surprising tenderness, her smile a cross between a Madonna's and a pixie's.

His eyes were closed.

"Good," she said. "It'll probably do him good to sleep."

We agreed.

She stroked his forehead reverently.

And then, as if she remembered she was not allowed to show emotion, as if she realized she had a reputation to sustain, she lifted her hand from his forehead and looked up.

"Miss Wragg," Swinton said softly.

But it was Hirsch's face she sought, riveting it with the blue bolt of her stare.

Hirsch stared back with defiance. There was still the glory in his eye and the blaze in his cheeks.

"Where does he live?" Miss Wragg asked, her eyes still on Hirsch, and her hand back on Ned's forehead, as if measuring the current between them. Her mind spun like the Isle of Palms Ferris wheel. "He can't stay here."

"He stays with his aunts," someone answered.

"The Confederate Home."

"Right across the street."

But it was too late to call them. Like all old ladies in the Confederate Home, Azalea and Eola retired early. I heard Swinton's voice.

"He has a studio there by himself."

"Well, see if he has the key."

Hilary went through his pockets. "Yes, ma'am," he called out, "it's here."

"Good." Miss Wragg was suddenly anxious. "Take him." She slipped his head from her lap and got up. She told us all to leave. She went into the hallway and switched on the light, she turned back and studied Ned. Undoubtedly, as she paced, she contemplated the exchange she had just seen. Pristine, serene, scientific, would be her contemplation of it that evening. I suppose she decided right then to see the thing out. It was not cruelty on her part, but a cold curiosity.

"Now you boys, get him up," she said, taking charge. "Be careful."

Hilary and Swinton lifted him.

I supervised.

"Grab him under the knees."

Some lifted and others reached. On a bed of outstretched arms, they carried him down her stairs and into the street. His lame foot dangled. She came downstairs and watched us leave.

I took the lead through the shadows, like jungle leaves where light was a machete. There was a *thump!* a *goddamn!* and the sounds of a near fall. I could hear Miss Wragg's gate closing. "God, Swinton, what's wrong with you?" Hirsch came up from out of nowhere. "Here," he said. "Give it over. Give him to me."

Hirsch followed me now, carrying Ned all alone, and he stopped in front of the door to the Confederate Home. "Wrong one," Swinton said. He motioned me down and gave me the key to Ned's room. After giving me directions, he ran away into the fog.

I called to Hirsch. "Over here."

Memory endows me now with a candle. I see myself carrying it aloft on the stairs; a circle of light follows up the wall. I look back: Hirsch has Ned in his arms: Abraham carrying Isaac to the slaughter.

As we crossed the deserted porches, yellow light looked out catlike through slits in the shutters. The rocking chairs swayed; a shawl rose up to dance, billowing about like a blue flame. I found Ned's door and opened it.

Shadows sailed in from the old-fashioned gaslights that lit the street. They disappeared as I hit the switch, and I saw that along the walls were crude childish swirls on cheap yellow paper. Ned's drawings jumped out at me in the glare of the electricity. I was dumbfounded. There were pastels on the gray walls and watercolors of monocled walruses, smiling sea horses, and jack-o'-lanterned trees, half-men, half-ladies. I saw boys become butterflies and begonias bloom into old ladies. Colors unfolded like a magician's handkerchief; and the room beyond was full of sculpture, a hall of tangled human forms. The colors on the walls were almost phosphorescent—shooting out like flares. The designs spun around the room and swirled in my mind like paisley.

"Hirsch, let's get out of here."

I had forgotten our tiff in Miss Wragg's hall. I was so naive I could not imagine drawing these things that did not exist, that seemed almost evil to me, a heresy.

Hirsch had carried Ned over to a cot. Having loosened his shirt, he was now crouching over him, tugging at his trousers.

"You go on." He undid the suspenders and sent them flying.

"No; I'll wait."

"Go on."

I stayed.

Hirsch turned; still crouched down, he looked over his shoulders and threatened like a dog, through bared teeth. "Get out of here. Leave us alone." He turned back to Ned and I waited. Then he stood up and turned around. I held my ground as he approached me menacingly. "Your presence is no longer needed," he said. Ned moaned and it seemed he opened his eyes, then shut them again when he saw me.

"Ned," I said, "are you okay?" I made a move.

In that instant of taking my eyes off Hirsch, he rushed me; he shoved me up against the door frame, and then hurtled me through it. He took one last look at me before shutting the door. His eyes were crazy. I had to catch my breath; but meanwhile, I heard the key turning.

"Hirsch," I started to whisper, scratching at the panel. "Let me in." I beat my palms softly on the door. I wanted him.

"What's going on down there?" A woman's voice quavered from a porch above me.

I panicked.

"I'll call the police."

Just then the moonlight touched me like a cold and ghostly finger and it made me jump. I ran down the porches and into the street. Hilary and Dwin had said they would wait; but they were gone, so I was alone in my vigil. I waited for Hirsch to come out but he never did. And, when I eventually went home I was too upset and pent up to sleep. I needed Hirsch badly.

That next day was terrible—gray, cold, and rainy with a dampness that crawls into bones, creeps into clocks, and warps more fragile things, like psyches. Like a living thing, the old museum building shuddered with each blow from the wind. All day long we had to run around with tarpaulins to keep the rain off the exhibits; it fell in great big drops that dribbled down from the leaks in the skylights high above us; when the wind got under the cloths, it seemed the whole building was sailing.

I was deadened from lack of sleep and could not keep my mind off Hirsch. The way he strutted around the building was too much for me. He must have passed my doorway a dozen times that morning. He was walking around like a new father—and you half expected him to rush up to you, hand you a cigar, and demand to be congratulated for his prowess. It was as if he had just won an award. Passing my doorway, he smiled in. And I smiled back. Tit for tat. It was disgusting. Miss Wragg noticed at the morning meeting. Though she had scarcely welcomed me back to work after my having been sick for two weeks, she lavished attention on Hirsch.

"You seem to be in fine spirits for such a glum morning," she said over coffee.

"I slept well," he answered.

"Oh?" She looked at him and smiled. "Any word on how that boy is . . . what's his name?"

Miss Wragg had an exceptional memory; but she was going to make Hirsch say it—to see his expression when he did. "Don't you know?"

"Swinton said his name was Ned."

"Ned what?"

"Grimke," he almost whispered.

"And he lives with his aunts?"

"Yes, ma'am."

"Phone him, please." Hirsch looked panicked; but Miss Wragg missed that, as she was suddenly all business and efficiency. She turned to her secretary. "See how he's doing, Miss Richardson"; (the museum was filled with women.) "And if he's up for it, ask him if he won't come by and see me. Tell him to bring his portfolio with him, too," she called out after Miss Richardson had disappeared. "Swinton said something last night about his drawings.

"Did you notice anything about them?" she asked Hirsch.

"Not particularly."

"Oh?" She looked at him with quizzical brows that relaxed, "Aha," as she smiled. "But you must have had your mind on other things." The silence was distressing. "Well," she said a minute later, clapping her hands together and going on as if speaking to children, "since it's not a good day for visitors, let's see if we can accomplish something."

We scattered in our different directions. That day lasted forever. We had to get the museum ready for an invasion of school children to come at the end of the week. They expected a puppet show, for Washington's Birthday, I think. So I went rummaging through the museum's collection to see what I could find. I'd have to make a marionette, I decided, and that didn't make me happy. I didn't like children especially. Besides, someone had toyed with my puppets in the room we reserved for the theater and tangled all the strings. I spent my morning working them free. I was still at them when I looked up and saw Ned Grimke in the vestibule. He did not see me.

I think he would have come even if Miss Wragg had not called. Like one of those figures in a Venetian clock, Ned, at his aunts' insistence, was used to appearing a day after a fit, and going through the mechanics of an apology. Azalea and Eola had taught him the proper things to say on such occasions, which he would recite as if from memory. For days sometimes, Ned was half in, half out of the trance, still a creature with no past, no memory. He had to remember who he was, crawl back into and claim the hollows of his body.

I closed my door partway so that I could see him through the crack every time he passed. As if through a gun sight, I lined him up. He could not see me. He had color in his cheeks and though he was obviously nervous he smiled occasionally, a smile you smile in memory of some pleasure, a smile that changed his face and made me angry. He put down his portfolio and smoothed back his wet hair. He looked so sharp and expectant.

He looked at the board that displayed our office members. He gulped when Miss Richardson appeared.

"Mr. Grimke?" she asked.

"Yes." It was obvious he was not used to being *mistered*.

"This way," she said; and Ned picked up his portfolio.

He was so apprehensive about seeing Miss Wragg that I almost laughed. You would have thought he had an appointment not with her, but with St. Peter, and all eternity hung in the balance. He limped along behind Miss Richardson and I followed them. Would Miss Wragg's door be open to him in the future? he wondered. Would she accept his apology? He wiped his perspiring palms on his jacket again and again.

Miss Richardson tapped on the glass; and Miss Wragg called out, "Come in."

She stood from her desk, and walked over, eyeing Ned coolly. They didn't shake hands and Miss Wragg half circled him, continuing to eye him over her glasses as if he were a specimen. How would she classify Ned, into what category would she place him?

"Are you better now, young man?"

"Yes, ma'am," he said, "thank you."

She said nothing.

"I wanted to tell you how sorry I am for ruining your party."

"What's done is done."

"Yes, ma'am," Ned said penitently.

They were silent. "What's wrong with your foot?" she asked suddenly. It was so brazen; it was as if she was questioning the color of his eyes.

"I was born this way." He spoke as if he were guilty.

"Walk around," Miss Wragg demanded.

He circled her, clip-clopping on the hard wooden floor like castanets.

"Can you lift things?"

"If they're not too heavy."

"You'll have to practice," she warned him. She seemed annoyed. Miss Wragg took the limitations and failures of all her "boys" personally and it was apparent that Ned was on the verge of becoming one. But she had to test him first; she took off her glasses and tapped them against her cheek, gazing at him. Then, "Catch," Miss Wragg called out suddenly. She had reached into her desk drawer and swiftly produced a small rubber ball that she kept there for just such an eventuality. She bounced it across the tabletop at Ned and he reached out and caught it with ease. "Quick thinking," she laughed. "Toss it back." Ned did. "You'll do," she said, smiling.

It was then she came up to him and shook his hand; she told him to have a seat and she closed her door. Through the glass I could hear her inform him in a rush of words that it was a shame; they were doing wonders with clubfeet these days; it was her motto of sorts, and she told Ned, "All hope lies in technology."

I moved casually away from the door. A few minutes later, when Miss Wragg opened it, I had my back to the files, pretending to be in search of something. Miss Wragg saw me but said nothing. She led Ned out; and I heard their voices echoing in the vaulted space as she gave him a tour of the building. They disappeared into the bird hall and then a great peal of laughter rose up. "Smart boy!" Miss Wragg cried out. "Exactly." I was in front of the shrunken heads when they reappeared, and I heard her say, "It's settled then; Cro-Magnon, Neanderthal, Phoenician . . ." She counted them off on her fingers as if she were summing up progress or conjuring the species. "So you'll do one for each civilization."

"Yes, ma'am!" Ned stood there smiling under the great skeleton of a whale that hung down from the museum's ceiling.

"You can go now," she said, but he remained, staring at her. "Did you forget something?"

"No, ma'am," Ned said, flustered.

"Well, what is it? If you're worried about the money, I'll make sure you get the figures."

"It's not that," Ned said. And the idea came to her and to me simultaneously.

"Aha!" she cried. "You want to see Hirsch Hess, don't you?"

Ned broke into a big smile. "Yes, ma'am; is his office . . . ?"

"Not so fast, young man," she said. "Remember rule number one? No friends at work; you're not on the staff yet."

She was firm yet gentle. But underneath you could tell her mind was busy. "I'll be sure to tell him you were here."

"Please. Do. Tell him I want to thank him for last night."

Thank him, indeed. I was so mad I could scream. He had come here not to apologize or to see Miss Wragg but to find Hirsch Hess. That's what made him so apprehensive. "You're not going to get him," I thought.

When he was on his way out, I turned back to my office. But I almost ran smack into Hirsch. He had been standing a few feet behind me.

"What are you doing?" I asked; but he did not answer. And he did not have to. It was obvious that, like me, he had been secretly studying Ned and Miss Wragg, and he made no bones about it. He did not even try to hide it from me. It was obvious that he had been waiting for Ned to leave.

"Going out tonight?" I asked.

"Maybe," he said.

The front door of the museum shut behind Ned; together we watched and I think we were both relieved. I took heart. Hirsch did not seem to like him; not really. He seemed keyed up.

Miss Wragg returned from the vestibule and seeing Hirsch, she smiled like a mischievous child hiding something. She motioned. "So there you are, Hirsch! I wondered where you were. You must have been hiding."

She laughed; and without letting him respond she summoned him. "There's some more paperwork for you to attend to; oh, you'll probably lecture me," she sang out, "but I don't care. I know we can't afford it; I've just got the museum another employee.

"Don't you have anything to do?" She changed her tone for me.

"Plenty," I said.

Her door closed behind them and I went back to my room. I was so upset that I broke the puppet I was working on. I threw it in a corner.

"Take that," I said, then retrieved it and stuck a pin into it and made it into Ned Grimke.

omething happened then. I could not get the idea out of my head that Ned was trying to snatch Hirsch from me. It ate at me all day, and, like the rain, it would not let up. With the sound of the rain drumming on the roof, I thought I would go mad. When I left at five it was still falling.

By supper, the rain was mixed with sleet; my mother suggested that I stay in, but that didn't slow me down. I went out looking for Hirsch, but he was not in the Alley. I waited until ten and then gave up and went back out into the sleet. On my way home, I passed by Miss Wragg's house on Chalmers Street. Her front lights were off, I saw, but in the back, between the slats of shutters, I could see her bedroom lights gleam; she needed very little sleep. I sometimes think that the rationality she championed balked at the illogic of dreams. She was probably up thinking over what had come to her the previous night. Lust or love? Damnation or delivery?

She vowed she would discover what it was she had seen between Hirsch and Ned. Walking along, I suddenly realized where Hirsch must be, and so I went down to the Battery, for that is where you turn, as if to a best friend, when you are troubled and queer.

But Hirsch, I discovered later that night, had no thoughts of going there. All day long I had watched him as he paced at the museum. I knew he must have been thinking about Ned. And going back to the Confederate Home that night, he, no doubt, walked along like an executioner to someone's last dawn. This time, it'd be different: he'd show that queer.

Hirsch was, after all, in his twenties. So there was no reason to hope; no reason to fear. Hirsch was so sure he knew everything about himself, his past, his present, and what his future would bring. He had no reason to worry. But why had it been different last night with Ned Grimke? There had been the pleasure of oblivion; he had found release. For some reason he did not feel guilty.

Pushing himself onward thought by thought, he realized he had to make sure that it had been a fluke. I suppose he had to make sure that he'd receive his punishment for being queer. He would. Tomorrow there'd be no reason to worry.

The outer door of the Confederate Home was always locked at six, so Hirsch had to hoist himself over the wall and drop himself into the courtyard. In the damp, the scents were out; they would have been the smell of cedar, the scent of secrets, overpowering. He would have gone up the ramshackle stairway like a thief.

I was not there. I did not see; I was still waiting for him at the Battery. But I have imagined it in dreams, both waking and asleep, so many times that I feel sure of it. And I saw the aftereffects of it, too.

It was hot in Ned's room, so he kept the door open; a ray of light fell through to diffuse into nothing, and disappear completely as a shadow crossed it.

Hirsch tapped on the screen.

Shadows; the scraping of a chair against the floor; movement of forms.

Ned's voice cracked from disuse when he called out, "Co-ming."

In a second he stood squinting in the doorway.

Hirsch fixed his look in profile to be more dashing. Ned, however, could not tell. The screen held the light. It could have been the devil beyond the door for all he could see.

Hirsch was unexpectedly nervous. "Yesterday," he said out loud. "Last night . . ."

"Hirsch!" Ned opened the screen and cried out, "I'm so glad you came. Did Miss Wragg tell you? I'm too glad you're here." He held out his hands, and his eyes almost crossed in pure pleasure. There was a light in them, and he skipped back out of the way to allow Hirsch to enter. "Come on."

Hirsch tripped. "I'm sorry," he apologized, as he stumbled. He was sweating. The building was kept hot for the old ladies. The radiators rattled.

They shook hands.

They spoke simultaneously.

Words fell like splashes, noisily, and, soon, almost as effortlessly. Ned was laughing. Hirsch felt peculiar.

"Have a seat," Ned pointed to a scaled-down wing chair in faded red upholstery. Hirsch pulled it up, and before the silence could reassert itself, he forged through it. He looked into his hands as his voice cracked. "Strange weather, huh? I was just going home . . ."

"It *is* strange." Ned stared at him with wonder.

So there were crisp comments, abrupt questions, and brittle laughter apropos of nothing. But that passed so quickly that Hirsch addressed his plea to himself, "Help me." He bit his lip, looked in the mirror, and called it out silently. He saw himself storming the door of a castle, while at the same time calling for help from the tower's highest balcony. He felt like surrendering. He felt giddy. Then it passed. He was Hirsch again, only saying impossible things he'd never have let pass his lips before. And Ned Grimke, close enough to kill, was more than attentive.

Hirsch felt a twinge of horror: he—whose motto was *don't tell anyone anything*, had told someone of his secrets, his dreams. Like a dog in a fight, he had bared his throat, and now Ned could get him, could use this knowledge against him. Ned was draining it out of him, absorbing what he said, hoarding it. He sat there, silent, with his eyes cast downward, almost worshipful. Hirsch was used to boys hanging not on his words, but on his body. Time passed quickly.

Hirsch wondered when Ned would make the move. He needed a sign. Last night seemed a dream. All he needed was a hand reaching up his thigh, then he'd take over; he'd show that little queer.

But Ned's hands, though they darted and circled when he spoke, did not come near; they kept shaping an elusive spiral thing in pantomime: they drew out his desire. Ned gave himself over to Hirsch as he had to Miss Wragg, trusting him completely. Hirsch sensed it and was excited by it.

He would have taken Ned, but something stopped him. Ned was different, hazed in an unsettling nimbus. He wasn't

just any boy or body; he was a specific. That bothered
Hirsch. He shifted in his seat and looked around the studio
for the first time.

Like Ned, the room might have surprised you at first,
for it was not at all what you would expect for an interior in
such a forbidding building. It was very simple: the walls were
tongue-and-groove paneling, painted gray, white near the
ceiling, with dark-stained floorboards covered with fraying
grass mats you would find at a house on the beach. There
wasn't much furniture: a few odd chairs, shelves, a cot; one
old Persian rug stood out like a flying carpet in the center of
the mats. The windows were blackened. All around him
were Ned's peculiar drawings.

"They're nice; I like them," Hirsch said.

Yet all those snails, stick people, and jack-o'-lanterns
were not entirely childlike: Ned's creatures were at various
stages of undress; with bulging thighs and buttocks, and
lascivious grins. Hirsch glanced from Ned to a drawing of a
half horse/half fish, female and voluptuous, with purple lips
and nipples. It worried him.

But the new feelings swelled up again, and though
Hirsch knew that bubbles were made for bursting, he rose
higher and higher in one, as if he were in a different atmosphere, one of helium instead of oxygen. Hirsch began to
talk, and it was incredible: forgetting that there was an end
to achieve, he felt like the first man on the moon. A new
world opened up for him. He smiled at the drawings on the
wall. Again, he felt giddy.

Out here he was like a dog with one flea; only one thing
worried. He thought he knew his repertoire of emotions—
knew the feelings he was doomed to shuffle like a loaded
deck of cards. He was, after all, he reasoned, in his twenties
(old enough, surely). But this was new, what he felt for Ned
Grimke.

"When do you start at the museum?" Hirsch asked him
suddenly.

"Any day now. Miss Wragg wants a diorama for each
civilization."

"Hell," Hirsch sneered. "Civilization; we're just beasts."

"What do you mean?"

Hirsch could not see through Ned the way I could. To him, Ned nursed no secret thoughts, kept no pet theories. Hirsch talked on and on, seeing himself bobbing up and down and along the flood of years. It was up to him to show Ned the refuse, the mortal debris.

"And at Gallipoli, the Turks beheaded . . ."

Ned tried unsuccessfully to stifle a yawn. The bells of St. Michael's massed their chimes, bursting into midnight. Hirsch had fallen silent, the sleet had stopped, and Ned yawned again.

"Well, I have been going on," Hirsch said.

"No, not at all."

"Well . . ." Hirsch said, and got up. Silence intervened.

"Don't go." Ned reached out to stop him.

What's wrong, Hirsch thought, as he reached back. Ned's drawing seemed to tilt and the light dimmed on the ceiling. Their fingers linked and they held on to each other to keep from falling.

The same thought joined them, and when they moved apart, fingers unlinking, it was as if after the act of love.

"Do you have something to drink?" Hirsch asked. His mouth was dry; liquor would make it easy.

"No."

"Then come on," he said. "Quick." He had to move fast so as not to lose this feeling.

"Where to?"

"Don't ask. Just come! Now!"

Ned got his coat, and they ran through the freezing streets to the Peacock Alley.

They arrived with cold and color in their cheeks. Chicco jumped down from his stool and looked at them as if he were seeing things: he blinked. Hirsch usually contrived to arrive alone, leaving with a victim in tow. If

Chicco stared at Hirsch, he must have burned holes through Ned Grimke.

"So you're finding them yourself now?" the midget finally said in a voice that exploded like a sneeze.

Hirsch looked down at him with contempt. "Button it, Shorty."

"Introduce me," Chicco demanded, blocking their way. To Ned he said, "This is my place."

But Hirsch just pushed Chicco aside, enjoying his own cruelty; and Chicco enjoyed just as much shouting back, "Well, no drinks on me tonight."

"That's fine with me."

They walked down the mirrored aisle, Hirsch ahead, Ned slightly behind; had they looked in the panes, they might have seen the midget slinking behind them at a distance.

Hirsch flashed two fingers at the bartender. He nodded as they went by to find a table. There were some colored musicians with horns whose tinkerings filled the air.

The Alley that night was filled with people the likes of whom Ned had never seen. There were women in red, some wrapped up with bows like presents, some barely dressed; others with peculiarly hairy arms and cheeks. Lilac men ambled by, and a thin mulatto with the cracked yellow eyes of a dope fiend bowed low and swooped off his derby. "Good evening," Ned said.

"Don't talk to him," Hirsch warned. "No one does." They sat at a table and would have talked, but people kept interrupting.

"Who's your new friend, Hirsch?" a blond boy with no eyebrows asked. "Aren't you going to introduce us?"

Others sat down and thumped Ned on the back and invited him over to their table for drinks. I was not there, but I made a point of finding out about it; it was no trouble, for there was another crowd that Hirsch would sometimes sit with when we weren't present. (I'd not usually have anything to do with those sailors, cotton-mill hands, and boys from the borough, but these were no longer usual circumstances, with my wanting to find out about Hirsch and Ned.)

They liked him, at first, those other boys told me. And Ned took to them immediately, touching their baubles and glass beads and exclaiming over their bright colors, plumage, and cheap finery. He asked them where they got their stuff and they talked and clustered about Ned like chickens feeding, until one of the boys looked up and shrieked, "Oh do!" It was like a bugle being blown and all fell to attention.

"Look!" he called out. "Mr. Renfrew's coming."

Luden appeared as suddenly as a genie and their ranks split to allow him passage. He stood in front of Hirsch's table, an avuncular, slightly hunched form with the drooping eyes of a spaniel. Tufts of white hair rose up from the back of his neck. His hands dangled awkwardly as he smiled. "Here," he said, pulling a bill from his wallet and handing it to a blond boy. He did not look at him. "Go buy yourself something."

"Thanks, Mr. Renfrew!" The boy sashayed off and the others moved off, too, but not out of hearing. Luden Renfrew, if nothing else, was always interesting.

"Mind if I sit?"

Hirsch made a noncommittal hand motion. "Help yourself."

Luden settled himself comfortably. "I see you've made a new friend," he said after a minute; he rubbed his hand over his lips. "Aren't you going to share him with me?" Luden smiled and leaned over and smiled more. He patted Ned's hand as you do to a friend who is fretting.

Hirsch pulled away, but reconsidered; with an air of fatality, he introduced Luden to Ned Grimke.

"I'm having another get-together tonight," Luden whispered confidentially so that not too many others would overhear; "after eleven. Will ya'll come?"

"Maybe." Ned looked to Hirsch.

"Please."

Luden put some money on the table. Hirsch glared at him and looked back at Ned. Luden wasn't proud. "I've missed you terribly"; he took out another bill.

Hirsch looked him in the eye and then closed his hand over the money.

"Good." Luden patted Hirsch's hand and, noticing Ned's confusion, he said, "Cab fare." He winked and pushed back his seat. "Things should definitely be going by midnight."

"That's too late for me," Ned said when he was gone.

"Don't you worry."

With Luden off inviting others, Hirsch relaxed. The boys at the other table watched him. He spread his legs, nudging Ned's knee.

"Wanna drink?" he asked and looked at his lap.

Ned nodded and Hirsch got up. Drinking, Ned confessed to one of the boys at a nearby table, was like going too fast on the merry-go-round: you went back and forth between exhilaration and dizziness. They rolled their eyes at that, they assured me. They were not fooled, nor were they born yesterday. They saw through him as I had. Who did Ned think he was deceiving?

"I enjoyed last night," Ned said to Hirsch when he returned.

"Oh honey!" someone shrieked.

The other boys broke out laughing, but fell into silence when Hirsch turned on them.

"Can we do it again?" Ned seemed oblivious to what was going on around him.

People had begged, but Hirsch had never been thanked before. It seemed to upset him and he recrossed his legs awkwardly. Hirsch studied Ned's narrow tapered face, vacuous blue eyes, straw-white hair, and spare body.

Others in the bar were wondering too; could Ned be as innocent as he seemed? How could anybody? I set them straight the next morning.

When the bartender came up with their drinks, Hirsch handed him the wad of Luden's money.

"Let's get out of here."

Chicco had been watching them. When he saw them get up, he jumped off the stool and ran down the hall to the doorway. He grabbed Ned by the hand before he could leave.

"What did you say your name was?" he demanded.

"Ned. Ned Grimke."

The dwarf let go of Ned's hand and looked him over. They searched each other's eyes and then drew back. "You'll do," Chicco said. "Yes, yes," he continued with enthusiasm, even relish, "you'll do nicely."

"Bye," Ned called out; he had to run to catch up with Hirsch, who was standing on the corner. The cold had revived Hirsch. He was himself again, and looked at Ned hungrily. He leaned there, smoking his cigarette, seeing how it would be, actually visualizing it. That, along with the drink, would have swollen Hirsch's crotch, made him sweat and, at the same time, made him feel curiously relieved. Hirsch first saw everything in his head, planned out how things would be; and that's how he took the edge off experience. Ned would beg for it, Hirsch would oblige. He would have him, and then guilt would mushroom from them as, defiled by touch, experience would make rotted, unclean things of their bodies. There'd be no release, no pleasure, no beauty. Hirsch would be free once more, free to be himself, condemned by desire. That evening had been just a fluke. Hirsch pondered the familiar possibilities as Ned caught up with him in the street.

They walked, then stopped. Hirsch brushed at his face; a cold sting.

Ned looked up in wonder and asked, "What's happening?"

"I don't believe it," Hirsch gasped.

And it was truly incredible.

I had been sitting and waiting for Hirsch at the Battery. I had never seen it before. For the first time since 1899 it was snowing.

In our childhoods, we had heard of it, had gotten word of snow's existence in the stories our parents told us; we had pictures of the event handed down to us in the stereopticon views that we would look at in the front room on rainy days and Sundays. And it was very much the same thing: the faded gray and white houses through the stark trees, dark water; it fell in a fury. It melted on the water and cold air rose up like steam. My eyelids were frosted and my cheeks were stung, and it stuck, miraculously, to the grass, and held to the trees. It was all over the city. Miss Wragg once told me what deafness is—the silence of snow falling. But this silence lasted only for a moment. Huzzahs and hurrahs rose over Charleston.

In their nightclothes, in the streets, the ladies of the Market danced that evening: with each other, with anyone they could grab. They were waiting to catch whomever they could from the Alley.

"Oh, hold me, Sunflower; snatch me in your great big arms," a red-headed country woman in a loose yellow dress cried, tripping Hirsch up. "My toes is freezing."

For a moment they danced; but Hirsch was about as natural as a music-box figurine. He lost his bearing.

The whore he danced with lurched to a standstill, her arms still raised. Hirsch glared at her and she dropped them.

"I didn't mean . . ." she started to back away. There were hoots and hisses from the line of women. "I'm sorry . . ."

Hirsch was coming toward her, staring at her blackly. He advanced until Ned grabbed him by the arm. "Come on, Hirsch; leave them alone. Let's go."

Hirsch looked back at the woman over his shoulder. "Where are you going?"

"We'll go bike riding."

"That's a fool idea." Hirsch turned to him. "You can't ride in the snow, can you?"

"Wait and see."

Ned had a key to the Chalmers Street gate. They snuck into the courtyard of the Confederate Home and wheeled out two of the ancient iron bikes that the ladies kept under the stairway. They were kept for market day, when the ladies would sail through the streets like galleons, their hems clipped together with clothespins. Ned and Hirsch released them from the frames, and Ned led the way through the courtyard and back to the street. They walked to the corner before they got on. Over brick sidewalks, slick and icy, they went sliding.

Hirsch stood on the pedals and hunched over the front wheel.

"Huh! Look at this."

Ned had his feet over the handlebars. His club foot did not seem to hinder him. "Watch out!" he cried to Hirsch, who was aiming straight at him.

He swerved.

"Jesus!"

"Quick!" Hirsch tried to stop the bike with his feet and they careened.

Their bodies grazed each other's; they must have felt a tingling. Ned brushed Hirsch off as they stood up; and Hirsch smiled back at him. He looked at Ned and desire came into his eyes as the color rose in his cheeks.

"Want to go back in?" Hirsch asked.

"Let's go on," Ned insisted. So they got back on their bikes, and oleanders became pylons as they aimed at High Battery.

"Is that a snowman?" I heard Hirsch call.

"No! Look out!"

Without really seeing who it was, they waved at the man on the sea wall who reached out in their direction, frantically trying to capture them. But it was as futile as catching and holding the snow, or trying to hold on to your dreams upon waking. I know, for that man on the Battery sea wall was me.

I called out. Though I am no fool, sometimes hope gets in the way of good sense. Coming from the Battery, I had just given up on running into Hirsch when he nearly ran me over. "Hirsch," I called.

As he pumped the pedals, I could almost see the rhythm of his muscles beneath his clothes. How majestic he looked next to Ned, who seemed to have borrowed some of Hirsch's glory.

I watched them disappear, the snow slowed, and I stood there sad and empty. Then I started walking, looking at my feet until two boys passed me on the sea wall. They jumped

apart, but moved back together when they realized it was
only me.

Although I did not know their names, I recognized
them from seeing them in the Alley.

"Luden lives there," one boy pointed to a house across
the street.

"You sure?"

"Yes." He caught my eye, crossed the street, and looked
back at me. He turned to his friend and they taunted me
with twisting fannies. Then, unknown to his friend, one of
them looked over his shoulder and winked. I heard a metal
gate clang and then they disappeared.

I looked one last time; there was no sign of Hirsch or
Ned. All I had was that hollowness in me that the clang of
the gate had sounded, like a clapper in a bell. I followed
those boys across the street.

I had made up my mind in an instant. I would go in. I
had reasons enough, and now the chance. I would finally get
to see the inside of Luden's house.

But my heart was in my throat as I opened the gate and
strode across the black and white tile of the low grottolike
enclosure underneath the portico. I knocked. I would have
run away had the door not opened instantly. I went into a
dank front hall, heavy with the scent of furniture polish and
candle wax. I said nothing to the black man who had re-
ceived me, and he said nothing in return, standing there
almost invisible, a denser condensation of the darkness. The
whites of his eyes were mesmerizing crescent moons; and I
realized he was pointing to the stairway that, like a note
from a soprano, spiraled up into nothingness. He did not
look at me again; he just pointed, and I realized that he wore
livery that strained and stretched against his thick arms. For
some reason the sight of that troubled me.

I climbed the steps and heard the laughter of the two
boys who had preceded me. Further on: jazz on a gramophone; to lure me on there was the promise of things unseen. I passed two deep-set Palladian windows with their
banks of magnolia leaves, tapers burning in tall brass can-
dlesticks: these and the polished mahogany of the treads

made me think of funerals. The overall pull was not of sadness and loss, but of mystery. I was curious and told myself I could always leave.

At the top of the stairs, God, how my heart beat; you'd have thought I had just climbed the Statue of Liberty. I paused. Through thrown-open-wide doors I could see a fire in the polished black marble hearth. When I finally mustered my courage and entered the dim room, no one noticed. The room was hung in silks and sported shiny brasses from the Mekong, alabaster elephants, hothouse ferns, statues of Shivas turned into seven-armed candelabra, and stuffed heads, jackals and hyenas, along the walls. Despite the snow outside, in here it was warm and moist, junglelike.

As if underwater, men in all states of intoxication lay strewn across the leather ottomans and tassled cushions. There were at least a dozen, maybe fifteen. ("Even numbers are for dinner parties," Luden was to tell me, "and odd are for orgies.") All were aglow with the fire's reflection on their tawny and perspiring bodies. One man stood in front of another on his knees; some danced with their reflections. In front of a tall mirror I saw two men watching themselves. A pair of legs were raised and in the fire's glow I could see thighs thrusting. Everything around me moved, seethed, shifting continually like snakes in a pit. The sounds I heard were the sounds, not of animals, but of men with men in the motions of sex. I might have run if two hands had not reached around from behind my crotch and cupped me.

"Another young one."

I jumped.

But a tongue began to smooth my neck, while a shadow in front worked its hands up my shirt and framed my chest. I turned my face and the tongue slipped into my mouth; my pants went down; someone put his fingers between my legs and took my shoes from my feet. I panicked and struggled to get away. But they intensified their efforts on me.

"Relax; relax," a breathless voice whispered in my ear. Their strokes began to excite me. I began to pass into that haze—the color of flesh, the smell of desire, the slowness of dreams. With so many hands playing on me, I was helpless. I gave in as if to sleep. Never in my wildest fantasies . . . It was as if the statue of Shiva had discarded her candles and had come down from her stand to pleasure me.

We wallowed in an ocean of flesh as new waves of men came in through the door all night. I had never seen them before and wondered where they came from—New York? Or Charleston? For all I cared, they could have been from heaven, or from hell. They could have blessed or blasphemed; they would have their way with me. Passion made putty of me, as each new man who took my hand refashioned me to his liking. If I was no one by the end of the night, it was because I was everyone.

There was so much to discover in that haze of lust and degradation; even of decency. So much, that we fought against the morning, to keep the light, like a venereal sting, from burning. And it was not till then that I met Luden, though he apparently had been there all along, moving from group to group sampling, before lighting like a fly on what he wanted. He and I did not come face to face until light came filtering through the paisley silk that hung across the windows and billowed out like a desert sheik's tent from the ceiling. The room looked like a battlefield, the floor sticky with spilled wine and strewn with odd clothes and strangers' bodies. Outside the snow had stopped.

Clad in a yellow silk kimono, Luden, sleepy-eyed, picked his way over naked backs. He had a half-drained glass in his hand; his too-black toupee was topsy-turvy, and his sad hound eyes were in search of something. He prodded bodies with his toes. I saw his face was lined and fallen, as he glanced up and said, "You're awake!" in a low rumbling voice.

"Yes."

"Well, good morning."

I was surprised that he could say mundane things. The stories I had heard of him made him into a fiend. I guess I had expected every aspect of his character to have been eaten up, gonorrhealike, with lechery.

I answered him bravely, pulling up my knees.

"I've lost my sho-oe," Luden intoned. With his slurred

speech—he always talked like a drunk reciting poetry—I found it hard to understand him. He walked off and I exhaled in relief. But then he returned in a minute, carrying a snapped golden high heel.

"Found it," he said, sticking it in the pocket of his kimono. He picked his way over to the davenport and dropped down on it next to me.

"Don't know if I've seen you before."

I nodded nervously.

He sensed it, I guess. "I may be a lot of things, dear, but I'm no tale-tell," he said. "Don't you worry." He lit a cigarette and picked up an abandoned drink, checking it against the light to see if anything floated in it.

"Ahhh . . ." he said, and downed it. "Gin," he said, "I think."

He licked his lips and turned to me.

"You're young," he said, chucking me under the chin. "Poor thing." He continued to look at me and mumble things I did not understand; but I could feel the kindness behind it, and it surprised me.

"Be sweet," he advised me, after I got up to leave: "and no need to worry. You can sneak out the back way. One of the colored boys downstairs will show you. Wake them up if they're asleep. There's a door that will take you right out to Church Street."

Once dressed, I stood and thanked him, staring into his eyes that never seemed to close, or even to blink.

"You be sure to come back now," Luden said. He stood and walked me to the top of the stairs where we parted, kissing each other chastely on the cheek like two little old ladies who had just shared tea. As I descended he waved a hankie down at me.

My feet did not hit the streets after I left. I floated in a daze, directionless, all over the city, until the cold, like a needle, like a conscience, began to prick at me. I came down to earth like a balloon with a slow leak.

It was the cold; it was my conscience; it was what I had done. (Or was it the age I lived in? Was it the city?) Was it the Lord punishing me? For now I felt sullied as the snow on the streets. All night long, Charlestonians had walked on it, denying its wonder, its purity. I was probably diseased. Now I knew everything I had been told about queers was true. We were despicable beasts, not quite humanity.

I couldn't then, but have wondered since what would have happened to me had I not been born into an unresponsive era, into a disapproving time and to a doomed city. My parents had taught me to treat my flesh like a poor relation—definitely to be acknowledged, but not indulged. Would they welcome me home if they knew this about me?

I walked along and the sun rose. Through the clouds, it was weak and white, more like the moon, incapable even of pity. I ran into Swinton at the fish house on Queen Street when I went in to seek solace in coffee.

Penitent and penniless, I asked him to buy me a cup. I wanted to be consoled, as if my sin entitled me to a treatment of luxury. But he just stared into his own cup and did not speak. I grew angry.

"Swinton," I tapped him sharply.

He looked up and I repented right away. He had become a mockery of himself, pasty white; he looked unreal, frightening. His face was panic-stricken; but he smiled grotesquely.

"What's wrong?" I asked him. "Have you been up all night?"

"Yes."

"Studying?"

He shook his head no.

I sat and he put down his cup. He swallowed and made a false start. "I went to the doctor Monday."

I remembered; "At Miss Wragg's . . ." I said, but I could not continue; he had been so peculiar lately, and I tried to block out anything he could say. "You've been working too hard, Swinton. You should take a break." But he interrupted me.

"The doctor says it's only time." He looked away. "I'm going to die, he told me."

"No!"

He held up a hand to stop me from interrupting. "Let me finish." I held his hand and he clasped mine back as if it were I who needed the comforting.

"There's a tumor on my spine," Swinton explained; "though now it's no bigger than a pea, it'll grow," he said, "and keep on growing." The bell on the door rang; some people came in and I could hear them laughing.

Swinton let go of my hand and balled up his napkin and almost threw it; but he held onto it, unraveling its creases, flattening it, studying it like a map. He hung his head as if ashamed.

I studied that napkin as if its creases were the lines of his palm and I were a fortune-teller. The laughter grew louder and I felt awful. The bells on the door rang again. I looked up. It was like a slap in my face: Hirsch and Ned were leaving with paper cups of coffee.

Swinton looked up and saw them and threw the napkin in the trash can. "Don't tell anyone else; let it be just between us."

"I promise." I looked away in distraction.

We watched Hirsch get on his bike.

"I thought you two were together," Swinton said, dismissing his own mortality and turning his attention to me.

"I did too"; and then, "I told you I didn't trust Ned. He planned to take Hirsch from me."

Silently we watched Ned get on his bike too, as he finished his coffee.

It *was* a conspiracy. Even the elements and Charleston herself were now ranged against me. Corner after corner turning into tangled ways, as if lured into a maze, on and on Charleston had drawn them into the heart of her mysteries. It had snowed all night long; and when Swinton and I saw the sunlight hit the street, it started to rise up in vapor. The steeple of St. Michael's seemed to be burning. Ned and Hirsch looked back at one another and waved as they went off in their opposite directions, Orpheus and Eurydice.

We did not say a thing until Swinton whispered, "Do me a favor."

"Anything," I said, not really listening.

"Tell Miss Wragg for me."

✳

I did, and something in the tone of my voice must have sounded like I was blaming her for it.

"Are you sure you're well?" Miss Wragg asked. "You sound feverish."

"I'm just upset," I said.

I was. Yet I was lying. I was not upset about Swinton. I was more upset about Hirsch and Ned, and me.

I watched them that day at work and that night at the Alley. They came in together, chatting like old friends—as I had never seen Hirsch chat with anybody. It was so strange that it was obvious to everyone else, too, immediately. But I would not admit that Hirsch had given me up for him. Nor would I meet the eyes of those who looked at me in triumph and bitchery. Some boys there were nice, however; they came up and held my hand and talked to me with a softness in their voices, but those others! Their eyes lit with mocking mischief as they looked on Hirsch and Ned, and then smiled back to me. I almost preferred them because I could hate them and threaten "Just you wait" under my breath. I carved little figures of them with the knife the museum had bought for me. It was better than accepting the condolences of pity. I wouldn't let go. I held on to the idea as tightly as a visitor to a madhouse holds on to his sanity. I would get Hirsch back from Ned Grimke.

✳

One evening, I came early to the Peacock Alley. I saw Hirsch sitting alone and lowered myself into the next empty seat.

Hirsch didn't even look up at me; but I could feel him tense nevertheless. "What's doing?" I asked.

"Nothing," he said.

"Looks like you're waiting."

"Smart boy."

"For Ned?"

"Yes." He looked up. "What of it?" His eyes dared me.

I kept mine steady. "Nothing." I ordered a drink, and he declined an offer from me. I told him I was sure Ned would not be coming.

Hirsch didn't say a thing.

"Patience is a virtue," I said.

Hirsch looked at his watch and said, "I'm early; he'll be here."

When my drink came I sipped it and laughed. "I can't believe this." I looked long and hard at Hirsch, as if what I had to relate pained me.

"Hirsch," I said, putting the drink down, "I just can't believe it. If he can fool you, he can fool anybody."

He looked up sharply. "What do you mean?"

The snow had all but disappeared by then but we still spoke of it, loath to let go of anything that had come to us from out of the ordinary. I had told Miss Wragg about Swinton, but not a soul about my night at Old Man Renfrew's.

I sat silently and watched Hirsch light a cigarette. I asked him to light me one. He did, and handed it on begrudgingly. The look in his eyes was one of hope: he wanted to hear what I had to say. He wanted to hear bad said of Ned Grimke.

I could almost feel the weight of his thoughts, crowding out mine, pushing them away, yet I said nothing.

And not because I was considering. I had not come with any plan; yet I was suddenly a genius held spellbound by the ideas that came, as if by their own volition, to me. Like bubbles in champagne, they came. I could not stop their rising.

"I bet you thought Ned was innocent."

"Isn't he?" Hirsch asked.

"I used to think so," I told Hirsch. I was masterful. "At least until Dwin told me different."

"What'd he say?"

"Oh, nothing really," I answered. "And let's not judge," I cautioned; "because you and I both know nice people go there." I was very sweet. "That's where we met." And

I stroked him: where it mattered. "Dwin told me he saw Ned getting into someone's car at the Battery."

Hirsch sank back into his chair, exhaled smoke, and took a long sip from his drink. "I don't believe it," he said.

"Believe anything you want to, as long as it makes you happy."

He sank into thought.

"I had a hard time believing it myself," I said. "But I saw him there tonight, with my own eyes. I had to pick my mother up from the Walkers, across the street. And I saw Ned then, in a carload of queers. Colored ones," I emphasized. "You know Chicco won't let their kind in here." I finished the drink. "But if you want to wait . . ."

Hirsch breathed in deeply. He had really liked me all along.

I was calm. It was only natural. It was my due.

Hirsch put his glass down and laughed a brittle, abrupt laugh. "That lying little queer." Hirsch smiled ruefully.

I smiled back and tickled the inside of his hand. I was happy. And there were no longer any reason for him to hope or believe. Ned, he knew, was just as wicked as the rest of us.

I transferred my hand to Hirsch's thigh. We did not speak, we just got up and left together, before Ned could come in. I felt like a recrowned queen, or someone called back from the guillotine, as everyone turned to see Hirsch and me leaving the Alley. I nodded at my enemies but did not speak. We went to our old haunts on Berresford Street.

And if Hirsch was a coward that night, then I was his fear.

We could have gone on, if not forever, then at least indefinitely, had not Miss Wragg gotten wind of something. She called Hirsch into her office one day and told him to get ready. "I'll be coming for you soon," she informed him.

"Fine," I overheard him say, without apprehension.

Nor was I worried, not until I had waited for her to tell me as well, and she hadn't. Then I became uneasy. I could see from my window, and feel in the wind, that spring was coming, so it would soon be time for her to go rescuing again. I wondered if she would let me go with her and Hirsch as she had last year. I knew I would not be as shy with him as I had been before, as we went riding down those rutted dirt roads of the low country. Sun dappled the windshield; the air was cool. We were collecting.

"There." Miss Wragg would point.

And Hirsch would turn down, how many I don't remember now—countless old plantation roads marked by fence posts, festooned with creepers, sunk in morning glories, wrapped round with ivy. We passed the empty slave cabins with bowed floors and doors hanging open balefully; we glimpsed, between the trees, rice fields ruined by salt water; and finally we drew up in front of those somber and reproachful smoke-colored houses. We were silent, hypnotized by the motor and the sudden seizing heat.

We would get out of her car and stretch our legs. I see us scattering in different directions—me to the barns, Miss Wragg to the house, and Hirsch Hess to the fields, all without a word, as if we were removed from time, participants in a sacred ceremony.

Later, when we were done and the car's backseat was piled high with relics for her museum—fragments of pottery, tools, iron gates, and pieces of threshing machines—we'd turn into a setting sun, back to Charleston. I remember a doe in the road, that spring, her brown eyes filled with a serenity that pained. I had looked across a tomato field and seen a woman; she was young and white and she hugged herself as she sat on a log, rocking back and forth in some half-rapt state; a lock of her straw-colored hair had gotten free in the wind and a tall solemn black man held out his hand to touch it; but before he could, the woman stood up and put that black hand to her white lips and kissed it, hungrily. We went around a bend and I cried out; but they were gone. I still thought of them—black and white, and the doe in the road—and the rattlesnake—that and those other flashes of grim and terrible beauty.

I looked for Miss Wragg's car from my bedroom window each morning. I waited for the signal, but it never came.

And when I got to work one day and her car was missing from the lot, I was suspicious.

"Where is she? Where is Miss Wragg?" I demanded. People were lounging by the water cooler and dawdling over their second cups of coffee; they turned to look at me. There was none of that military precision we usually snapped to when she was in the building.

"Out," someone said.

I ran to her office. Only Miss Richardson was there, reading something. She crumpled it up when I came in. With a sheaf of papers like a palmetto fan in her other hand, she said, "She's gone out rescuing."

"But who'd she take?"

"Hirsch Hess."

"Why didn't she wait for me?"

"Don't get so upset," Miss Richardson soothed; "there probably just wasn't enough room."

"But there always was for three before."

"And that's how many there was." Miss Richardson smiled.

I must have looked puzzled, for, "She took that new boy along, too, the nice quiet one," she said. "With the club-foot. Ned something. You know how I am with names!" She laughed.

I said nothing.

"Is anything the matter?"

"Nothing," I said. I was so mad that when I went to my office to work, I broke the blade on the knife with which I had been carving. It *was* a conspiracy.

Every other day now, even before we got to work, they had disappeared, the new trinity: Miss Wragg, Hirsch, and Ned. But she held aloof from them; she knew her position, and would not tamper. They were her "boys," after all, albeit parts of an experiment she was conducting.

I was angry, jealous, and worried. All three; even

though Hirsch had himself told me how he'd deliberately avoid Ned as they rode. He'd drive and whistle to himself or draw out Miss Wragg with discussions of archaeology. (She, at least, must have been pleased to have someone to instruct, while observing gleefully to herself how her experiment was progressing.) Hirsch refused even to catch Ned's glance, he said. He sat there in the car a stingy Midas, refusing Ned even an accidental brush of his golden flesh. Hirsch was as stiff as a corpse with Ned.

He was angry with him and was punishing him for having raised his hopes, for having made him believe. He would make him suffer for it too. He'd get even with Ned Grimke.

This sure puzzled Ned. When I met them at the parking lot and helped them unload, I could see the confusion in his face. Hirsch didn't even say good-bye to him; he just went away with me.

"I like Hirsch so much," Ned confessed at work one day. "But he is so mean to me."

I looked at him once and that was all I needed. A hectic flush rose to his face and played, like blushes, all over his body. I could tell desire was having its fun, dancing through him like a disease. Ned moved his hand over himself with a restless energy.

"An itch." He shrugged.

"Oh?"

"Maybe poison ivy. Miss Wragg took us to Pon Pon and Hirsch was so nasty."

I said nothing.

"I saw the leaves along the path," Ned explained. "My foot caught in them and I knew I was going to fall. Hirsch held out his hand, but then he pulled back. Why is he being so ugly?"

Maybe he doesn't like you. I wanted so badly to say that; but my upbringing prevented me. Anyway, it wasn't necessary, for I knew it would be me Hirsch was joining after work.

"He's a pill," Hirsch would laugh and say as he puffed on his cigarette in that room in the whorehouse on Berresford Street. We lay spent after the act, looking at time's deposits, patterns of grime on the ceiling. "You can see right through him," Hirsch said and passed the cigarette to me.

"Dwin said he saw Ned coming out of Old Man Renfrew's house."

Hirsch started, but caught himself. "I hope he gets a disease."

"Dwin says he might have one already."

So I talked and Hirsch listened. And when the cigarette was finished he'd leave.

"Why?" I tried to draw him back, but it was useless.

"Have to wake up early," Hirsch would explain. "Miss Wragg is coming."

She came for him about five-thirty every other morning. She'd surrender the wheel to Hirsch and move to the passenger's seat.

* * *

✳

"Where to?" he asked one day as he got in.

"Secessionville."

"Coming up," and he put the car in gear.

The bridge across the river had not yet been built, so they took the ferry. Once over, Hirsch drove the car over the rutted wagon roads that deserted the river and took them deeper and deeper into the country. The sun was up. Birds sang, and alongside the road you could discern some glimmers of green spring's coming. Miss Wragg was involved with maps, occasionally glancing up to gauge her reckoning.

Soon she looked up for good and refolded the maps. "We should be there by now. Aha." A gatepost obediently appeared.

They drove in and immediately began their gathering; it was all Miss Wragg had hoped for and more, she said later. What a trove they amassed while the old gray wooden house of narrow windows stood aloof in the high grass in all its weather-beaten glory. She kept them busy. Scattered around the house, like a duenna and ladies-in-waiting, were the plantation's outbuildings: a kitchen, a barn, and stables. The three moved past them like gleaners through the fields, gathering up farm implements: hoes, rakes, onion-shaped bottles from the eighteenth century. The farm had the appearance of just having been vacated. "Are you sure no one's here?" Hirsch asked when they stopped briefly for the lunch she had packed.

"Not according to my research," she said, chewing her chicken-salad sandwich methodically. Miss Wragg pulled out the abstracts and handed them to Hirsch and Ned. "You boys look them over." Hirsch surrendered them to Ned, who barely glanced at them before passing them back to Miss Wragg. "Looks okay to me."

They soon went back to work, and Hirsch periodically glanced over his shoulder. One of the upstairs windows was open; white curtains beat in and out like a flag of surrender. Hirsch said later he could not shake the feeling that someone was watching.

Miss Wragg worked them all day until thunder rolled up from the river. They made the porch just as the big drops of a spring rain began falling.

"Want to go in?" she asked, prone, as ever, to her curiosity.

"Sure," Hirsch said; "if it's not trespassing."

Miss Wragg shook her head. "Who's to see us?" She turned the knob; the door was not locked and opened easily. Ned was the first to go in, but he stopped immediately. "It smells awful in there," he gasped, and hung back from the darkness.

"It's from being closed up," Hirsch said. "Don't be such a baby."

Miss Wragg went in after him, leaving Ned alone in the chill rain-dampened air. "I'll be out here," he called to them.

Hirsch had charged right in. "You can have the first two floors," he told Miss Wragg. "The best things are always in the attic," he said with authority. He climbed the two flights of stairs to where they ended in a gothic-framed doorway. The smell came in spasms, like pain. He pushed the door open, and stopped to catch his breath. He moved cautiously through the dark.

As he walked, dust rose up in little tornadoes around his

feet. Footprints led through it; someone had been here re-
cently. His senses did not rise; he had no warning. Across
the raftered attic, in front of a shuttered window, a silhou-
ette stood out against the weak louvered light. Was it a dress
dummy? A drop of rain hit Hirsch's cheek; he moved out
from under the leak and stopped.

The thing softly spun back and forth.

"Hello," Hirsch called out cautiously. "Anyone here?"
Hirsch too began to sway in rhythm with it.

The thing seemed to speak. *Shall we?*

He almost heard music playing.

Then—and there would follow a definite progression of
sensations as he relived the moment and told it again and
again to whomever would listen that night at the Alley—he
was aware of a surge in his body, as if his arm or leg were
asleep; a tingling. He could feel the tenseness jump his syn-
apses. He was about to be frightened; he peered through nervously. Then, *oh my God*, he thought, and his gorge rose, his
body preparing. But he hadn't enough time. The fear hit him
in a blinding flash. He said he knew what it was then: a
colored man spinning in a noose. He ran; by the time he
reached the second floor, his throat was raw from screaming.

His eyes had focused for a second in the dimness, and
he had seen the dead man's bloated disfigurement, and where
the rats had gnawed. Then he looked away in disbelief, then
back again, and so the dangling body seemed to come at him
willfully, swinging back and forth: the skull grinning with
the scream of a banshee. He felt as if he had been hit in the
face with it as he roared down the stairs from the attic.

He reached the lower floor just as Miss Wragg came into
the hallway; she screamed, too, when she saw him; she
reached out to claw his face; and he raised his arm to fend
her off. Still running, they tumbled together like tenpins.
The floorboards knocked the breath out of them. In the insanity of the moment, Hirsch looked out in front of him,
intrigued by two cloth circles that had fallen to the floor. He
reached out and touched one and then the other; he stroked
them with his long finger.

"She's dead." Miss Wragg raised herself from the floor

with her hands. She pushed back a strand of her hair and screamed "Murder!"

She had twisted her ankle and could not stand.

"In the bedroom. Over there."

Hirsch pulled himself up too; he heard music playing.

"The poor girl," Miss Wragg sobbed. "She's dead; and so is her baby."

But Hirsch could not listen. Miss Wragg did not understand; there was a dead black man in the attic and there was a stitch in his side from fear. He picked up the two folded cotton falsies.

"Help me up," Miss Wragg demanded, panicking. She tried to get to her feet.

All this time, like a cat at a mouse hole, crouched and imperturbable, Ned had been waiting on the porch. He jumped up when he heard all the shouts, the sobbing, and ran inside. From the bottom of the stairs, he looked up, and Hirsch Hess and Miss Wragg looked down on him, huddled together.

"Ned," she called out, sighting him; her eyes were pleading. She tried to stand but couldn't.

"What is it?" he asked.

She stretched out her hands as if begging to be pulled from quicksand. "Help me, please."

He ran up the stairs as quickly as he could and put his arm around her. Coming back down, Miss Wragg, with her blouse opened, leaned against him, panting; she limped along the hall and sat down in a spindly hand-carved chair. He patted her shoulder.

"Miss Wragg, what happened up there?" He looked her straight in the eye. "Miss Wragg. Tell me."

Her eyes slowly unglazed. She backed away from him. Shivering, she reached for her bosom, the sagging billows in her blouse. That brought her to. She sat up stiffly in the dark hallway. "We must call the police," she said, as she discovered the loss of her padding. Her eyes rose to the top of the stairway.

"Hirsch! Give those back to me. Do you hear me?"

Hirsch sat up at the top of the steps, clapping the falsies together like a wind-up monkey.

"I don't think he hears you."

"But he must." She buttoned her blouse. "I need them." She made Ned her deputy. "Go on." She pushed him to the staircase.

Ned crept up the stairs one at a time, with his arms outstretched, one in front, one behind, as if he were approaching a mad dog or a suicide about to leap from the ledge of a building.

"Hirsch," he whispered. "I'm coming; just give them to me, okay?"

Ned got as close to him as he dared. He felt ashamed for Hirsch, seeing him in this condition. The weakness did not become him.

Saliva spattered his lips and his chest rose and fell like a piston. Hirsch made gruff sounds and looked as he did sometimes when he alone saw something out of the corner of his eye. He was breathing noisily.

Ned looked down at Miss Wragg who sat, arms outstretched and palms open; and then back at Hirsch. She called to him. Ned held out his fingers as if scared to touch flame; he stroked Hirsch's cheek with a feathering motion. Hirsch turned his head slightly and looked into Ned's eyes with pure, naked fear. His lower lip trembled; and Hirsch shook his head.

Ned smiled tentatively.

"Stay away from me!" Hirsch bellowed, accenting each syllable clearly.

Ned collapsed against the wall. With a sudden leap, Hirsch fled down the stairs. Ned clutched the railing.

"Where is he going?" Miss Wragg called from her seat. She tried to get up to pursue him but fell back. Ned slowly came down the stairs. She reached out for him. "Ned," she called out desperately; "I need them back. Did he take them with him?"

"I don't know. I'll see . . . but first, give me your keys."

"Keys?" She looked at him as if he were mad.

"So I can get the police."

She reached for her purse. "But they're not here! I must have dropped them upstairs." She looked down the hallway. "That poor girl," she said. "The poor baby."

Ned went up again and the smell met him. He knew it was death. There was a colored man in the attic, a white woman in the bedroom, and their baby. He found Miss Wragg's keys in the bedroom doorway.

Outside once more, he breathed in. The sun was setting. I know he did not have far to go. I retraced all his steps the next week. Against the clearing sky, he would have been able to see the telephone poles loom up. I myself followed them, like stepping stones, to a farmhouse, stuck in the thicket of trees like a stone in a plum.

Light blazed in the windows when I drove up; forms popped out of the darkness and hounds began to bark. No one seemed surprised when I said why I was there. I accepted a cup of coffee. I asked them to tell me about the boy who had come there before me.

"We told him there was no use calling the city police," the man with the light blue eyes of a weimaraner said. "They wouldn't come, we told him. We'se County."

He had asked him if they were dead. "No chance of being mistaken?"

Ned had shaken his head impatiently. "Well then, boy, what's the hurry?"

Ned had asked if they would call the police.

"Sure; I'll call them, son," the man answered. "But God's law and man's law," he told Ned and he told me, as I was getting into my car, "remember, they's two different things."

When Ned returned to the house it was ghostly in risen moonlight; the clouds moved back for a moment and shadows reabsorbed it. Miss Wragg was sitting in the parlor; from somewhere she had procured a kerosene lantern and had lit it. She was still on the same chair, but in possession of herself again; the strands of her hair were wound up in a bun; her dress did not hang loosely. She sat as erect as a Victorian spinster, patting her hair. Ned was awestruck. It must have been painful; she must have crawled on all fours and searched the stairs and hallway to find where Hirsch had dropped her falsies. But apparently no price was too great to pay for her dignity. He blushed as he looked at her blouse.

"Did you call the police?"

"Yes, ma'am."

"Good," she said; "and please be careful not to touch a thing."

"Have you seen Hirsch?"

She said nothing.

"How's your foot?"

"It's my ankle," she corrected. She flexed it and winced. "Sprained, I think."

They waited.

Ned paced and Miss Wragg watched him. "You know," she said, "it's funny how quickly we get superstitious." She pulled her sweater around her shoulders and her voice dropped. "Just thinking that they're up there, upstairs . . ." She broke off and continued in a different voice. "It's terrible how a couple like that has to exist in fear." It was as if she was having a conversation with separate halves of herself. "You don't suppose they were murdered, do you?

"Of course not," she answered herself; "no one would; it was just a lover's pact."

Ned got up. "I'll go see if the police are coming."

"Fine," she said. "I'll be here waiting. But where else could I be?" she asked, giggling a little hysterically.

Ned went out the front door to the high bluff above the marshes and breathed in deeply. Beneath him the grasses stirred; the river was rising in a bright tide of light. He looked up and clouds fell away from the face of the moon like rotting rags; stars now spangled the great gray oaks whose black masses rose up stark and wet in the darkness. Their branches arched and curved back down to the ground, touching it, like great arms laying down a burden with an ancient graceful weariness. And there was a burden in those trees: from the depths of a rope hammock in the branches, a red cigarette end gleamed. Ned approached and saw it was Hirsch Hess.

It was so beautiful here, Hirsch was thinking, a warm night . . . the tide and the marsh brimming in moonlight. Beyond the trees the battle for Charleston had been fought. Hirsch and I had helped map the locality for the museum. Secessionville, 1862. Four hundred unremembered souls now lay in the next field, the bones of those lost in the conquest of the city. And now her lights gleamed across the creeks in victory. Even in the darkness the green of the field gloomed, for human tragedy had enriched the soil, bringing a great beauty; a wisdom bloomed here. Those lovers in the house, dead, disfigured, disgusting, those lovers had lain in this hammock, Hirsch thought; right here, in love and ignoring the wrongs of their ancestry. The love they had shed, like the phosphorus of sea creatures, like animal heat, seemed to linger here. Hirsch lay in it and was comforted. He hung suspended in time and in the tree.

Inside the house all was complexity and horror; but here, outside, it was calm, uncomplicated, easy; he breathed deeply. Would he have to go inside again? he wondered; why couldn't he stay forever out here in the warm evening? He knew why, and it made him feel like crying. It was because he was Hirsch Hess, and like the house, he had his own inescapable history.

He sighed; and the love of those now dead lifted him. *If only*. The tears finally came, brought back like souvenirs from the battlefield. *If only*. Now he was weaponless and stripped of the armor of his ideas, shivering in his own mortality. Hirsch lay in the hammock with no battle plan, no future strategy. He was alone. It was that; and the tide was turning, rushing in to fullness only to be betrayed by the cruelty of the moon. The tide could not be held against the shore forever, but, with time, it would return to the sea, and the marshes would be nothing but muck and rot. The smell of departed life hit his nostrils in a nauseating sting. Light came through the trees like a message.

It seemed to surround Ned and to be thrown back from him as he walked along. "Don't be frightened, Hirsch," he called. "It's me. Are you all right?"

"Yes." Having raised himself on his elbows to answer, Hirsch fell back in the hammock, stung.

Why was he damned? He looked at Ned and remembered their first night together. Why couldn't he relax? Anger took so much energy. He thought of his parents and a marsh bird cried; a fox had got it; or one of its newborn. The ache in his throat cramped him and he balled up into a knot.

Ned came up and Hirsch looked at him. Then he held out his arms.

"Hold me. Please." Hirsch was ready; it was the moment, not Ned. If not for Miss Wragg, it could have been me.

He spread out the rope knots of the hammock like a web. There was no shame, only the essence of pleasure, its evanescence, as Ned crawled in. Ned reached out for him and, spun in a cocoon, they clung together. Their lips were not limits, and they melded into one another. Only souls could search so deeply.

As they lay together the love of those gone seemed to sough through the trees. There were footsteps, something was approaching in the moonlight. They jumped up from the hammock.

They were ready for ghosts, but it was only the police. Hirsch moved away from Ned. They followed the police back to the house, where in her circle of tricky lamplight, Miss Wragg sat waiting.

She took charge then, supervising the answers to the policemen's questions. I was told that they were neither curious nor shocked; they went upstairs and looked and came back down. They wrote down answers. Hirsch kept his distance and tried not to catch their eyes; he was afraid they could read his queerness, the illegality of his psyche, in his face. Ned, however, kept coming forward, and Miss Wragg pushed him back. "Be quiet," Miss Wragg would say as she played with the buttons of her blouse. "Stop fidgeting."

When they were released by the police, she had Hirsch drive them back to town. "I'll go to the doctor tomorrow morning," she told them. Hirsch and Ned carried her up the stairs to her room like a goddess. She kept them there for over an hour. They talked over cups of liquor-laced tea, trying to make sense of the tragedy, but it didn't take much imagining, for all the pieces were there: a white woman, a black man, an unborn baby. "Definitely not murder," the police had told them at the house. "Suicide," Miss Wragg now said with authority.

They talked like fever victims, deliriously; and the mere speaking seemed to purge the horror from their memories. When Miss Wragg dismissed them with an official thank you, Hirsch and Ned went without thinking, without speaking, to the Peacock Alley. Only our deaths, falling in love, or Sundays could keep us from the sentence we were compelled to serve out there nightly.

When I came in, Hirsch was sitting at a table. I could tell something was up immediately.

He was silent, seemingly at peace, mulling things over. Dwin told me everything excitedly. Hirsch nodded at all the details, exhausted from his own retelling of them. Hirsch seemed dazed; he had receded.

He was not the Hirsch Hess I knew; nor did he seem to know me. He was only half in our conversations and kept his eyes on Ned, who flitted about like an insect.

And that was not like Ned, now all adrenaline and intensity. He looked people up and down as they came in; unable to sit, he stood and shifted from foot to foot as if crawling with ants. "What's wrong with you?" someone asked.

"I don't know," Ned answered. "Something's got ahold of me."

"Well, whatever it is," Dwin said as he brushed himself off, "it better not get on me."

Hilary got up to fetch our drinks.

"Nothing for me," Hirsch said. Swinton slipped in quietly and took a seat. Ned drummed his fingers on the table as colored people's music climaxed and crashed around us. "What would you call that, Swinton?" Ned asked.

"Jazz," Swinton told him. "Haven't you ever . . ."

But it was obvious to us that Ned was no longer listen-

ing. He had ears only for the tones that rose like a reptile
from a charmer's basket. He cocked his head and listened as
if someone were calling him from far away. I remembered
how he had turned his head to listen to his invisible friend
Jervey.

The music called out to Ned, provoking him.

I had been to a revival once, and it was of that this
most reminded me. As if called to an evangelist's platform,
Ned rose and limped up to the dancefloor. But the dancefloor was deserted as the other boys left it. They made way
for Ned Grimke.

You could watch what happened as the spirit seized
him. His eyes swirled and his features twisted; he began witnessing. He moved his hands in front of him like an Egyptian in a wall painting. Then he looked at Hirsch and moved
his hands up and down his thighs with a saxophone's slow
urgency. The music climbed, and it was not a snake at all; it
was a spirit in search of a body.

Hirsch's and Ned's eyes locked; in the cacophony, you
could almost hear ancient voices shrieking down the centuries. Salome was dancing in the Alley.

Ned rose up in front of us like a flame, expanding with
melody.

We were too stunned to say anything; then Dwin shook
his head and muttered, "Dancing like that is bad enough;
but to dance alone!" He clucked his tongue. "It's just like a
darky."

"Not so fast, Dwin," Swinton said. "Do you see what I
see?"

"What?"

"Look," he said. Ned was holding out his hand to
Hirsch, who was actually getting out of his chair and going
up to join him.

"I don't believe it," Swinton said.

"What?" I asked. "Swinton!"

His eyes were luminous, his skin translucent, he seemed
to be glowing. I had told Miss Wragg of Swinton's illness and
now she would have nothing to do with him; she did not
believe in the efficacy of suffering.

We watched Hirsch get up and dance with Ned. Swinton let out a low whistle. "I think Hirsch Hess is falling for Ned Grimke."

I turned back to watch them. And I don't know what worried me more: that they were dancing the Charleston together or that they were doing it without me.

Beyond the pale, and beyond our limits, we watched them leave. And they were as together now as surely as if they had taken vows.

They had made it across the border, were smuggled to the time that exists on no calendar but is the product of movement, like time gained traveling at sea. They had made it into lovers' territory.

I think we all tried to follow them in there; all of us tried to climb after them like Romeo on his trellis; but in those coming weeks none of us succeeded. Envy is not the most substantial of frameworks. But then neither is truth; or history. Neither of them has ever been able to provide those boys with what they want, those who come to me from the Battery, who come accusing. They say they want the truth; they say they want history; but it does not satisfy. All they really want for me to do is gild the lily of Hirsch and Ned's lovemaking. They expect a string of scenes of Ned and Hirsch together, the boys at the circus, the beach, looking for bargains in the flea market all underscored, of course, by musical themes, as you would have it these days in the movies. The music for Hirsch would be something from Rachmaninoff, no doubt, full of dark power and a melancolic brooding that breaks, sunlight through clouds, into melodic rhapsody. As for Ned, they are not sure what they want to hear. Something pleasant—perhaps Musak—with no triumphant highs or lows, dentist office tunes, easy listening. That, or the jazz notes that he had danced to in the Alley. But I can't provide any of these things; I am no musician. The truth intervenes—it is the bane of stories. I have to tell those boys, when they come here, that Hirsch and Ned were too far gone; as soon as they were in the water, they were drowning. Even if they had wanted to dawdle, I don't think Hirsch was capable of it. The rhythm he had pounding in his blood was *suffer, suffer, suffer*: but quickly, too. He was in a hurry. But after their first night together, there wasn't much to see.

I know, for with both of them working at the museum, Ned on his dioramas for children and Hirsch with Miss Wragg's complex classification system, I was with them every morning.

✳

I suppose Hirsch must have instructed Ned how to behave, how not to smile too much, not to blow kisses and such things. They had grown together so quickly that they seemed almost inseparable. They were playing a game, a cross between charades and blindman's buff. Ned did not ask why, and now when he looked at me, there was contentment in his eyes; they were no longer searching.

They played well. I watched them but was not fooled, for at night I saw the blindfolds fall at the Peacock Alley. But Miss Wragg didn't. I wonder if she guessed what lay behind the charade. She had broken her ankle at that house in Secessionville, and so, for a while, she had to be content with what she could observe from her office. She remained there all day, having reports brought to her from all parts of the building.

She had not been born to sit still. After a week she had her desk taken into the main exhibit hall, where she was carried like Cleopatra. Sunlight poured down from the huge skylights and she sat surrounded by her relics. Like moments, the dust motes fell; she sat enshrined like a bronze through all the centuries. She had a little bell that she could ring when she wanted something. From where she sat, she could watch all the visitors and see into the bird hall, the Egyptian Palace, and most of the other galleries.

Miss Richardson would come when the bell rang, and that was often, for whenever restlessness or curiosity or evil got the best of her, Miss Wragg demanded to be rolled in that large white wicker invalid's chair that she had rescued on one of her missions. The fanlike back spread out behind her like a collar. Miss Richardson pushed, and she steered. You could hear the batlike squeals of her rubber wheels approaching.

She entered Ned's room periodically; he was, she noted with satisfaction, finished with the depiction of cavemen; Phoenicians were next, and already he had molded little Egyptians and pyramids and palm trees. You could watch history progressing in clay figures.

Miss Wragg would sit in judgment, shifting her headquarters there for an hour or two.

"Bring Hirsch to me," she'd demand.

He'd enter briskly with the notebook, nod to Ned, who'd smile back, maybe wink, and go on working.

She watched them impatiently for a clue but none was forthcoming. I wonder if she could tell what was going on nevertheless, and if she did, her wisdom did not come from experience: it came from intuition or theory. To Miss Wragg love was like sudden death or tragedy, the type of thing that happened in tabloids to someone down the street, but never to oneself. To her love indicated a breach of etiquette, a lack of breeding.

I sometimes suspect that the reason she conspired to match Hirsch and Ned up was for the same reason my cousin Shan would take me to the beach on Sullivan's Island in the spring. He'd stand on the shore and hurl me into the waves; I'd come up choking, gasping, with salt in my eyes and lungs, and there he'd be, hands on his hips, wanting to know how cold the water was, whether it was comfortable enough for he and his friends to go in swimming. But while he was cruel, Miss Wragg was curious. Cautious. She wanted to test this idea first; perhaps she thought love could be disfiguring.

So they played their game and she watched and perhaps she was fooled, for as I say, they played pretty well and every day they improved. But their house of cards tumbled whenever they accidentally touched each other. Then it was panic. You could see them jumping apart so fast it was as though they were at the same magnetic poles.

Afraid of getting overwhelmed in the attraction, Hirsch would blush and ignore Ned and start speaking of something totally unrelated to anything. His voice got high and his palms and forehead sweaty. If folks could murder a colored man and a white woman, he wondered what they would do to queers. He knew, as well, that Hebrews were not liked here. He did not want a soul to know that he cared for anyone outside his family.

Miss Wragg would smile at them as they pulled apart, and then Miss Richardson would hear her bell ringing. Miss Wragg would be rolled away, the rubber wheels of her chair squealing.

*

After work, Ned and Hirsch went home in separate directions. Charlestonians ate dinner at two or three in the afternoon then. Late tea or light supper came in the early evening. The Hesses did not follow our custom, and ate their main meal at night.

Mrs. Hess would perch anxiously on the edge of her seat, looking at Hirsch as he swallowed each mouthful. Was it good? Was it too dry? How about gravy? Mr. Hess did not speak at all and steadily devoured his food.

On the wall, a gaudy Hansel and Gretel clock dutifully ticked off the seconds. If you looked in through the frame of the windowpane, the Hesses resembled some macabre spoof of a family. They did not speak and if you crept to another window, near the oleander bushes, you could hear the clock tick. Pressed closely against the grimy pane, you could even see Hirsch's face. But he did not see out. He stared anxiously at the clock on the wall. Soon it would be time to meet Ned. Darkness would be swirling down the alleys. When the clock rang eight, he would excuse himself; he'd carry the dishes to the kitchen as solemnly as a pallbearer. Then there would be the silent mouthing of farewells, sometimes a kiss, and he'd leave.

Once outside, he'd look around. He'd gulp for air as he proceeded down the street. From a distance I'd watch Hirsch

approach each reunion with worry. There was that half second, as he saw Ned waving at him from the post office corner, when it seemed he was capable of doing anything. He
might even bolt. I guess he thought the attraction would
evaporate in the interim and that idea appalled him. The
attraction was real, he knew, but he never dared describe his
feeling. If forced, he'd admit, "I'd like to be with him," or
some such thing, using the lesser charged words of a lover's
vocabulary. Hirsch was rightly suspicious of this feeling. If
you happened to see him on the street that time of evening
he looked as if he were on his way to the guillotine. Three
and a half hours had passed since he had seen Ned at work.
That was time enough to wash away the euphoria and re-
place it with that dull grayness that clung to his parents. Mr.
Hess silently brooded behind his paper, just enough of a presence to be aware of, and Mrs. Hess, with her suspicions and
imploring blue stare, sometimes made you want to tear your
heart out. How could a son of theirs be happy?

Hirsch was silent when he first joined Ned. They fell
into stride, and Ned babbled on about his dioramas, his
aunts, his drawings, anything at all, it didn't matter. For
Hirsch was not listening. He was peering into himself, to see
how the change to come over him would occur.

Have you ever watched moonlight on water? Light caps
and then loses the tops of waves, like countless electric eels
appearing and disappearing. You can see it today from the
Battery; and you could have seen it then in Hirsch. One
second he'd be morose, then he'd be afraid, and in a moment's flash he was smiling: he was the person he'd become
with Ned; a different person entirely. He was volatile and
disconcerting.

Sometimes I could hear what they said.

"Have a good supper?" Ned would ask.

"Yes."

"And tea?"

"Fine."

Ned had invited Hirsch to the Confederate Home one
night to meet the two tall old ladies. The sisters Azalea and
Eola (I could not tell which was which as I watched from the

porch) seemed as fine and faded as the lace they wore on their collars. As they poured tea and passed points of buttered toast, they spoke of the birds and butterflies they had seen that morning.

"Sister, I'm sure it was the red-throated we saw in that tree."

"It was not; you should wear your spectacles, dear."

"But," the other reminded her sister, "you borrowed them from me this morning."

They had been together so long you could not tell where one began and the other ended. With them it was funny, but not so with Hirsch and Ned; they were becoming more and more like each other, and less and less like us the longer they tarried in lovers' territory.

I could feel the change in atmosphere as they lingered in the Alley when I came in and sat with them. And so I was brought within their circle. But I was always pushed back out of the warmth, which was worse than never having felt it. They needed me like Isaac needed Ishmael. In this world, they could tell each other everything, their wishes, their fears, and even their histories. You could hear them chattering all the time. It must have been difficult for Hirsch to lay out all the monsters and beliefs that made him; it would have been the same as unwinding the strands of his nervous system. But he did it.

Then, after a drink or two, they'd go up to the dancefloor. People stopped what they were doing. It got to be a ritual for others to come to watch. Even strangers came. Some praised the "modern" quality Ned's clubfoot gave those dances. Others came to steal Hirsch's eyes from Ned. But they failed. Would he ever be soothed again, led to forgetfulness? Hirsch wondered. Death may be Lethe for us; but passion for them was Nepenthe.

❋

I watched them once at the Fayssoux House, at one of the first concerts of the Spiritual Society. We sat and watched the first half as the descendants of plantation folks, dressed in hoopskirts and Prince Alberts, sang the old Gullah spirituals abandoned by the blacks who had inherited them. The Society had just been formed and was quite a novelty, by no means near the fame it would reach as they sang before presidents and toured the country.

Miss Wragg had sent Ned in some official capacity to arrange the costumes and lighting. She had given Hirsch the keys to her car to drive him; she insisted the car be of use to somebody. "You can keep it the weekend," she told him.

It had nothing to do with me. I came out with the boys who were in charge of supplying the bootleg; Hampton's Rye is what it was called. And I think all of us were drunk on something that night: some with each other, some with the night, most of us just feverish with the whiskey. The blacks of the neighborhood stood under the trees, respectful and keeping their distance in the darkness.

A moon had risen while we listened, shedding a pale light over the grounds, bringing the house and forest into relief. It cast a luminescent glow over the costumes. It was warm. Spring was coming. Lanterns hung from the trees and there was a slight smell of kerosene. I had pulled my blanket near to Ned and Hirsch's, and sat entranced, moved by the weird sounds and the soft beauty of the night. In the first half, Ned had tapped his foot to the shrieking tunes that doubled in overlapping rhythms what they lacked in melody. The moon pulled on Ned and made him restless.

"Is it bothering you?" Hirsch asked in a tone of voice he'd never used with me.

"Yes," Ned answered.

"It used to bother me too," Hirsch said; "it was like ants in my pants and made me crazy."

"Why?" I interjected.

Hirsch and Ned looked at each other, then they looked at me. They broke out laughing. Ned whispered in Hirsch's ear.

"Wait," Hirsch said. "People are just getting funny."

Again, Ned whispered.

"We will, I promise." He touched Ned's lips with his finger, sealing him to silence. Ned gave me a smug look. "Sit here."

The moon rose higher and trickled down through the trees. Its light spattered Ned and seemed to burn him. "Oooh," he called out, jumping up, "it's all over me."

"Sshhh . . ." Hirsch pulled Ned to the shadows, then they reappeared.

"Moon," Hirsch shouted, pointing at it with his cigarette. "Stop it; pick on someone your own size. Quit bothering Ned."

But it shone forth.

"Let's go," Ned pleaded.

"Just a little longer, okay?"

Ned pouted and looked sulky. He squirmed as if insects were biting, though it was too early in the season for that.

In a few minutes, he disappeared.

There were people there I knew from Savannah and we sat together under the trees, eating boiled peanuts and talking. I told them I was thinking of moving back there. Pretty soon, the colored women in the distance began to speak in loud whispers. I almost thought I heard my Dah's voice.

There was a great rustling in the tall hedge across which the lantern shadows bantered in confusion. Then the green broke open and a magnificent creature appeared.

It stood tall, splendid, and erect; its antlers tossed the air, and its mane was like a beard that cascaded down its gleaming white body.

"Oh my God," Hirsch said out loud. But he checked himself. He watched half in pleasure, half in fear.

Others gasped, pulling back their daughters. They were too shocked to speak, never having witnessed one of Ned's dances in the Alley. Even Hirsch and I were surprised by this one, for Ned had somehow secured a wreath of leaves and a rustic G-string, and only that and shadows cloaked his body.

He moved closer to the light. Sticks were his antlers, his mane, moss. Some thought him a character from Shakespeare's *Midsummer Night's Dream*, but the word got out that night that there was something peculiar about Ned. He moved on through the shadows of the trees as if he knew them intimately. He had a set of quills, like Pan's, and played a little melody.

He danced like a satyr on arched feet, up to an old lady from the Confederate Home.

"Fool," she screamed, and shooed him away with her skirt.

Ned pranced around, trying to entice her, but she clutched the shawl around her shoulders as if it were the mantle of her respectability. She took a jab at him and he laughed.

The tune on his pipe suddenly lilted, then ceased, and he stuck the instrument behind his ear. He stood in the clearing, scanning all our faces. He paused on mine, but Hirsch's was the one he fixed on. He laughed a fine resonant laugh, sure of himself. His eyes held the same challenge they had once used on me. He crooked his little finger and mouthed the words "Catch me." Then his arm arched upward; the other arm followed and he salaamed the moon three times before he swung up in one of the downreaching trees and disappeared.

A hubbub rose from the crowd; the singers launched into the second half of their singing.

Hirsch and I took off in search of him.

"I don't need your help," he said; but I ignored him.

We wandered down the mazed and interwined gardens, boxwoods rustling in our wake. "Ned," Hirsch called out. "Ned." That lament was eerie in the breeze. I can still hear him calling. It was my Dah who taught me that there are souls lost in the wind. "Listen," she'd say, and sure enough, I would hear shrieks in the air, howls and curses in the chimney. I sometimes still hear Hirsch calling.

"Where are you?"

We came upon a statue of a Greek girl, pulling a splinter from her foot. Her eyes were pupilless, as if turned inward on her sepulchral beauty.

Camellias reached above us, high as trees. Soon the paths diverged. Hirsch was first to find him in that clearing. The moon peered through, highlighting an old marble crypt against which Ned leaned. He laid back in a delirium; moss straggling down from his shoulders, his antlers at his feet; the leaves had disappeared. He watched Hirsch's approach without fear. Ned raised his arms as Hirsch reached out for him. It was a magisterial gesture, and heeding it, Hirsch kneeled.

Ned took a step or two forward. Even limping, he was regal. They did not see me. I was riveted, watching.

Ned was slim and lovely and blessed; his body looked like a crude medieval crucifix in the moonlight, all plains and hollows, though built for pleasure, not agony. All three of us were sealed in a circle of silence. I closed my eyes as if to receive the sacrament. As Ned approached, Hirsch kneeled.

I could hear, through the trees, the grotesque and melancholy wailing of whites singing like darkies. "Twilight of the gods" is the phrase that occurred to me that afternoon as I saw the sliding golden sunlight pour through the gray and green of trees, burning in their leaves, urging them on to glory. "Twilight of the gods" is the only way I can describe the feeling that was roused in me. It was so gentle, sad, and peaceful. I could not be jealous.

We were all enveloped in a warm, calm magnificence that soothed like music, unlocking the soul to melancholy.

*

"What do you think you'll be doing in thirty years?" Hirsch asked.

They sat on the marble stoop in front of the monument; Ned held his blond head to one side and ran his fingers through his hair. From time to time his eyes glowed eerily in the moonlight. I could feel them moving.

Ned smiled in wonder as if he had never before tried to second guess the future.

I had once asked Hirsch the same question in our room on Berresford Street. He had just grunted. "I'll be sad and tragic," I told him. "A lonely old queer, fat, with a high-pitched voice like Hilary's; I'll probably wear lace panties and drool over the boy who delivers the groceries."

"I want to be happy," Ned finally said to Hirsch. "And you?"

"I'll probably be miserable. I'll do something awful and you'll hate me."

"Don't say those things. Spit and say you were only fooling."

I listened for a while, but soon I could hardly hear what they were saying. I got up to leave.

"Don't look," Hirsch cried out a moment later, shielding Ned's eyes, ducking. But there was no need to fear.

It was not their foe; it was not the idea. That crashing in the bushes was just me.

I could not stand to see them anymore. I had to get away. I ran to my car and drove back to the city.

Luden Renfrew was throwing a party.

I knew Hirsch and Ned were beyond me so I gave them up. But Miss Wragg persisted. She forced her car on Hirsch when he tried to return it after the concert.

"Go on, take it. But keep it in good repair." She pointed to her ankle in its cast. "With me like this, that car may as well be of use to somebody."

Hirsch thanked her and watched her eyes as she handed him the keys. Was it sarcasm? Or cruelty? Or maybe they had acted so well in front of her that she was fooled and did not know what was transpiring. As she passed him the keys, she smiled and patted his palm.

"Why don't you take a pretty girl out riding with you this Sunday?"

"I sure will," he answered, and winked.

He and Ned fled that very next day. We rarely saw them after that—even in the Alley.

It seemed, as I sat at home at night, that time was carniverous that spring, eating holes in hope, devouring with worries. It ate at Swinton but he never complained. He seemed to be disappearing. I visited him when he was too weak to come out, and still he counseled me. I was no longer jealous; I was bitter and empty. For satisfaction there were the men at Luden's, or strangers on the Battery. I felt I was going backward, falling into some hole, while Ned and Hirsch were hurtling forward with breakneck speed; and Ned seemed to be leading, pulling Hirsch on into some new world he had wanted to enter for so long, his fearsome world of fantasy. Days were a blur as spring advanced and greenery filled the city; exotic flowers raised their heads in swamps and along the streets. Vague dreams and fears kept me awake, and ghosts glided between the trees of the Battery.

Every day Miss Wragg's machine conveyed them further and further away from Charleston. When the familiar roads were used up, Hirsch took Ned to savage, windswept places. They went rescuing one day, they told me, to an old chapel of ease on the river, a brick, high-pitched hip-roofed building built early in the 1700s. Thick white shutters sealed the windows, which were the only breaks in the mellowed reddish masonry.

The nearby plantations had been swallowed up; there was no more gentry to come down by river barge on Sunday. Talk ceased once out of the hissing automobile; they walked, cowed intruders. The graveyard on a high bluff of the river was overgrown with brambles. Tombstones rocked; there was a sound of clods of earth dropping into the water.

Hirsch went up to the doorway; he pointed.

In the bricks were the initials of the architect and the date he had finished the building.

Hirsch pushed the door open with a shoulder. The interior was revealed in a cast of weak sunlight.

Inside wasps droned along the coves of the vaulted ceilings, filling the air with litanies. There were the original pews painted white for the whites, and tan for the servants. They tiptoed in. Ned was disturbed by how the church, existing in its abandoned state, didn't need human visits to realize its beauty. But he was startled to hear himself say, "I don't like it. Hirsch, let's get out of here."

When they went back to town, it was only to sleep. Every day, with an air of ownership, Hirsch would unravel vista after vista of forest and savannah and ruined rice field, which in their rolling on seemed to say for Hirsch, whose chest swelled with pride as they were revealed, "I live here." Hirsch never took him to Mazyck Street.

Talk was rare as they hurtled down those roads with a desperate urgency. I saw them once as they returned to town, careening around the corner into King Street. It was as though they'd be perpetually young, their bodies bent forward in excitement. Charleston reached out after them, but they escaped. The time that passed in Charleston was not for the living, but was the time of museums and mausoleums, redolent with death and dampness and old ladies. How they must have panicked, condemned to return, when Miss Wragg began to draw in the boundaries of their territory.

"Who did you take riding with you?" she demanded of Hirsch one Monday morning.

"Did you take a pretty girl along?" Her voice lifted in a lilt. "Or was what I heard right? Did you take Ned Grimke?"

She laughed and Hirsch did not answer. Miss Wragg picked up her bell and you could hear it ring all over the building.

＊

That afternoon Ned came up to Hirsch.

"Want to go to the Greek's for coffee?" he asked.

"No," Hirsch answered loudly, in a stranger's voice.

Ned stood there puzzled.

"*Move*," Hirsch whispered tensely. "Get away from me. I'll explain later."

As if sprayed with poison, Ned wilted instantaneously.

But he had had to do it, Hirsch told Ned later that night as they rode. And the next day, it was even more necessary. On the bathroom wall he had seen where someone had scrawled their initials linked in a heart: HH & NG. Now it was out in the open.

Hirsch panicked even more when Miss Wragg asked for the return of her car. They were marooned in Charleston now, and he avoided Ned at work. They passed in the halls without speaking.

Once that began, it was only in the darkness of the park
or bars, or by the light of the moon, that he'd dare to see
Ned. They did not see me.

But Ned did not seem to care or take notice of anything. As long as Hirsch was there, he was happy.

And there seemed to be no regret or sadness on his part
when their evenings would pass and he was no longer with
Hirsch. When Hirsch left him after love, he was somewhat
surprised at finding himself Ned Grimke again. He would
drift through his mornings at the museum. When he was not
with Hirsch, he was like an unused toy.

But Hirsch was worried. He looked over his shoulder
now and watched everything and everybody suspiciously.
When beset by a thought, he did not let it go. He would
probe it, turn it inside out and back again, examine it with
his close scrutiny and still not let it alone, but then force
possession of it. Who had written their initials on the wall?
And why had Miss Wragg taken back her car? Why couldn't
Ned face these things too? Hirsch got so tired that he grew
angry.

And it *was* his fault; Ned was responsible for the guilt
Hirsch had felt at having to sneak around the museum, the
streets, the whole city; for had he not made Hirsch happy? If
Hirsch had not changed, people like Miss Wragg would not
have turned their heads and looked at him peculiarly. Had
he not been so nervous and upset, there would not have
been that scene in the Peacock Alley.

We were sitting there one night, playing cards.

Swinton and I were partners against Hirsch and Ned.
Swinton shuffled the cards and dealt them out deliberately.

It took patience to play with him. "Go away," we
wanted to say to Swinton; "die by yourself." But we couldn't
do that. We had had the "proper" upbringing. So instead we
sat and played our hands as placidly as if nothing were out of
the ordinary.

"Oh, Hirsch," Ned sighed once as he played a card; he
clucked his tongue in mock severity.

Hirsch grew rigid in his chair and snapped, "Don't you
Oh Hirsch me!"

There was no mistaking the ugliness in Hirsch's voice. I could see a vein in his forehead throb.

Ned looked up, puzzled. He parted his lips to speak.

But before he could, Hirsch bellowed, "I don't want to hear it." He threw his cards down. "If you don't like the way I play, leave."

"But I don't want to go," Ned said, as if this were a game.

"How would you like to suck peter at the Battery?" Hirsch said in a singsong voice.

"What?" Ned seemed too stunned to say anything else.

"I know you've been there," Hirsch said, "people have told me." He then accused Ned of every perverse act, every position in the Kama Sutra, every conceivable infidelity.

Swinton and I looked down at our laps as the torrent ran on.

Ned smiled tentatively, like a stranger being addressed in a language he'd not mastered. "Who saw me there, Hirsch?"

"Who? Does it matter? I hear you've cheated with almost everyone here." His eyes now cried out for help, as if fighting some demon that had taken control. "I've heard you've even done it with colored boys," he jeered. "What do you need? The cannon in the park?"

He leapt behind Ned's chair; with a loose wrist and a sashay he imitated Ned's limp. "I'm real loose, please diddle me."

That did it. Ned was bolstered by his love for Hirsch, and I think he could have taken abuse from him until doomsday. But with that imitation of his odd lope and walk, he blanched. He stood; his chair fell over; he was sweating. Ned lunged to escape.

"Oh please," Hirsch taunted, "you gotta stick that big black thing in me."

Hirsch became an image of himself twisted in evil mimicry; his face grew more cruel as Ned ran out of the Alley.

"For God's sake, follow him." Swinton tugged at my sleeve.

So I went out after Ned; and like Scarlett O'Hara, who

never had a handkerchief, I am never quite prepared for crises. (When *Gone with the Wind* was published, Hilary and I would weep over it, ruining 10,000 hankies.) I was not prepared for the night's wan serenity. From somewhere nearby I heard Ned sob.

I called out and found him leaning against a warehouse. He slid farther into the shadows as I approached.

"Don't go."

Then my voice cracked and I was not unaware of the irony. "Ned," I said, as if I were his best friend. "It's me."

I suppose he was curious. He did not run; he turned.

With no light, his face seemed featureless, his tears had worn him down to nothing. The tears stopped but his nose continued to run. He wiped it with the back of his hand, like a kid.

"I hope you'll drop Hirsch," I said. "Get rid of him. I'd never let anyone treat me that ugly."

He sighed and slid his hand deep into his trousers pocket. He seemed to be considering.

We stood still for a while saying nothing. Then we walked down the street and turned down one of those utility lanes that run between buildings. He stopped and looked in front of him.

I reached out to touch him, to comfort him.

"I didn't do it!" he cried. "Not with anyone but Hirsch; I swear."

I tried to say something, and again he misunderstood me. He turned on me like a cornered animal, eyes shining and teeth clenched. "You make me sick!"

"But Ned."

"Don't you touch me." He dodged me and ran back inside.

I vowed then never again to lay a finger on Hirsch Hess or Ned Grimke. I would leave them alone; and I did. I kept my distance, which was difficult, for they were coming more and more often to the Alley.

I saw them there every night, and Hirsch was never again so ugly. When anguish and self pity got him again, he fought it back. He'd be gentle with Ned all night, quieting the vulgar, shielding him from what others had been saying. And they had been busy. Stories had spread like vines whose tendrils had worked their way into cracks, into the consciousness of the city. Someone was making it his business to abuse them. Hirsch made sure that Ned never heard any of those tales that were circulating. As they prepared for an upcoming fete, tacky little queers with souls the size of a flea's would get together to scheme out of pure spite and jealousy, and rumors were rife in the Alley. "Don't sleep with him," one nellie boy would say to another.

"Why not?"

"Why, I've heard he'll rot your you-know-what off as fast as you can say sodomy."

Like vultures, they curled their painted fingernails around the railings of the bar, and watched Hirsch and Ned.

When Hirsch and Ned left the Alley, they wandered the streets of the city.

✳

I happened to see them early one day at the yacht club. Hirsch hung back, but there was no reason to worry. There were sailors among Ned's kin; he had been out in the harbor with them dozens of times before, but for Hirsch, the city might just as well have been landlocked. He balked, at first, but Ned convinced him. They borrowed someone else's twelve- or fourteen-foot boat and pushed it into the breeze, the sail unfurling.

Crouched beneath the boom, they sped across the sparkling water. Not to Fort Sumter, the fortress of rubble that birthed and buried, and is now the symbol of Charleston's history. Nor did they spend their time watching the skyline. I am glad that they had one more day free of all the steepled shadows, and the ghosts in the streets. As I watched from the dock the sea swelled gently, but not enough to make the bells of the buoys toll. Overhead the gulls seemed free of the wind, buoyant, circling effortlessly. Every once in a while, they dove for the bread Ned tossed them. Hirsch and Ned caught each vagrant breeze and tacked across the blue. Hirsch was learning names of ropes, the difference between rudders and tillers. On land, he would have been ashamed to admit ignorance, but now he learned painlessly: how to get where he wanted to, how to have the wind work for him, and that the world did not cease at land's end.

Words were not used out there; they would be snatched away by the wind, churned up by the sea. There was no room for them in the aching blue.

Even the sky disappeared as they lay flat, sails wrapped, with their eyes closed. The sun pulverized all thoughts, warming their browning bodies.

I saw the sheen of sweat on their bare bodies, and I sensed a harmony between their breathing. I left them to get ready for the Peacock Alley's party.

How could he see them

✳

We had been busying ourselves for it for weeks, ransacking our parents' attics for costumes—for hoopskirts, Confederate uniforms, old silk sashes, fantastic hats, and fabric. We pondered the placement of each strap and button as if our fate depended on it. I tried on my harlequin suit three times that day to make sure it was okay. After leaving the Battery I changed into it again.

Once in the door of the Alley, I was relieved no one had challenged me on the streets. I showed my invitation to the doorman, and he waved me by. In these past few weeks, my face had become so familiar here that even in costume, wearing the superb black and white papier-mâché mask that Ned had made, I was recognized by almost everyone.

Going down the mirrored hall, I ran into elves and sprites and fairies; there were tomcats and knights, pirates and stevedores, Southern belles and Yankees. Dwin and Hilary had corked their faces and come as Uncle Remus and Aunt Jemima. They came in laughing.

"Oh, Dah."

"Bad chile." Dwin tapped me. We started speaking in Gullah and people flocked around, laughing at our darky stories.

When Hirsch and Ned came in a few hours later, their faces were still fresh; they brought the harbor wind with them. But that was not why the doorman did not want to admit them. He pointed out the line in script at the bottom of the invitations. "Can't you read?" Ned stepped back to let Hirsch forward. "It says 'Costumes Only.'"

"Come on," Hirsch cajoled.

"I'm not kidding." The doorkeeper crossed his arms and stood in front of them, guarding the door like a genie.

"Come on, Hirsch." Ned pulled at his arm and edged away.

"How about this?" Hirsch pulled away from Ned toward the doorman. He took his shirt off and handed it to Ned and reached for his.

"No," Ned protested, crossing his hands over himself shyly.

"Come on," and he pried Ned's hands away from his chest and started unbuttoning. "Don't be so shy," he said. They exchanged shirts. Hirsch turned to the doorman.

"And who the hell are you supposed to be?" he asked.

"Ned Grimke!" Hirsch opened his eyes and smiled. "And this is my friend, Hirsch."

Ned glowered at the doorman, then broke into a smile. "Out of my way," he said and pushed gruffly past the doorman, who called out laughing, "You win."

They came down the narrow hall with a burst of balloons and confetti. As usual, everyone turned to watch them that night, for they stood out even more—the only unmasked revelers at the party. We were the dreams and they were the dreamers. Hirsch towered above everyone; he moved through the crowd gracefully and easily. He strutted as if proud; he came through the room with his arm around Ned, who looked more than ever like a waif in Hirsch's huge billowing shirt.

Luden Renfrew, dressed as Zeus, came up to take their hands. He was handing out small thunderbolts and money. "I want to invite you . . ." he yelled; "I want to invite you both . . ." He wrung their hands.

But it was impossible to hear; he stopped; he set them free. He pushed them onward. He gave up and winked at

me. "Will *you* come?" he said. The band had just broken
into a Charleston; there was a sound of corks exploding.
Hirsch took Ned by the hand to the dancefloor and we followed, watching.

There was a ruckus at the front door, but with all the
shrieks and noisemakers and music and dancing, it was hard
to tell what was happening. People were being pushed into
the back of the bar, as if the whole building had suddenly
tilted. We were being jostled and herded together; people
argued as they bumped into each other, spilling their drinks.

"Something's gone wrong up there." Dwin craned his
neck back to see.

I suppose those on their side of the law had been preparing for weeks, biding their time, gloating. They wanted a
show, and they waited to catch us all in our queer panoply
and pageantry.

They broke in the doors. I was in the back of the bar, so
my first warning was a scream. I still don't know whose it
was, but I suspect it was Chicco's. Like a crack in a glass, it
spread. The music stopped; and we were caught like drunk
men in that curious gap between thought and action. We
stood packed, one against the other, spilling out into the
dancefloor. Hirsch and Ned stopped dancing, like figurines
on a wound-down music box. A streamer fell. The crowd
started muttering, and Chicco, grotesque and half undressed,
came running through with wings askew and eyes popped
wide with fear. He was a pink cupid trailing multicolored
bunting. This was his birthday party. There was a smudge at
his mouth that we knew was not lipstick.

No one said a thing as he flew by us. We looked at him
and we knew. Since we were not expecting a visitation of
the Lord, we knew the police were raiding the Alley.

We panicked. Chicco raced by us to an unused door,
and he clawed at the clasp with funny upturned fingers until
it swung open and he was swept away, weightless, into space.

All at once, we lost our paralysis. We could see the
police pouring through the arched doorway. Those sitting
jumped from their seats. A whistle blew, and we all screamed

and stampeded. We clawed and scratched and fought each other for the doorway.

The police came in, drunken and reeling; they had picked up some volunteers, Irish firemen from down the street and a few folks from the League of Decency. They came in with a spray of obscenities, shouting, "Get 'em! Get them fancy boys!"

"Catch him; tonight's open night on queers."

Some boys were trapped in corners and dropped to their knees.

"Let me go," I heard one boy scream. "I'm not one; I'm just visiting. You know my father . . ."

And then there was a policeman's laugh as the boy was jerked up out of his chair and, like a marionette, he danced with him in a waltz of brutality.

One side of the bar was plunged into darkness and the piano exploded as something collapsed on it. Before the lights went off altogether, I saw Hirsch and Ned duck out the door. Something grazed my ear. Glass smashed; there was a scream. Caught in the tangle of those escaping, I stumbled out through the doorway.

Arms reached out after us and a young boy was yanked back, screaming, by a policeman.

Hirsch shoved Ned ahead of him, shouting, "Go on"; a fleeing form snatched at his arm. I saw Ned's face, white with fear. He was pulled away down the alley.

A voice through a megaphone yelled at us to stop; and in the sudden glare of a searchlight beam, we froze. And then we queer boys ran down the alley like roaches scattered by a light at night.

Ned had had a head start. I knew it was he up ahead by his odd, crablike way of running.

I caught up with and passed him. Hirsch grabbed his arm and half dragged him along, and for a moment I could hear them right behind me, the counterpoint of their odd breathing. But they began to lose ground.

"Please Ned, faster."

Then they picked up speed and were about to pull up alongside me, but I saw them disappear. They had fallen, tripped by a drain that caught Ned's heel. They lay crumpled in the street.

I halted and went back. "Are you okay? Get up; come on; the police are coming."

Hirsch raised his head and shook it, looking up, unaware of the fact that he had nicked his forehead and it was bleeding. Though I watched his expression change as he rose, it was not until Ned had scrambled to his feet too and we three were running again that I understood all I had seen. Once standing, Hirsch had smiled; and the look that came to his face transfixed me. I saw his eyes clear of pain and his mouth drop open as if he saw a miracle. I think he saw himself go back in time, go across the sea, so that he was with his parents being chased by a mob down the ghetto streets. His eyes lit with glory. This was the moment for which he had yearned and of which he had dreamed so often that it seemed a déjà vu to him now that it was here.

He stopped and cried out something I could not hear, for sirens and shouts and footfalls echoed eerily in the alley. Triumphantly, with tears in his eyes and smiling, Hirsch started back in the direction of the police.

But Ned cried out.

Hirsch stopped and looked back at him, confused. He made to move again but touched his hand to his forehead and examined his bloodied finger wonderingly. Then a whistle screeched and Ned grabbed him. In an instant the three of us were running again.

There was a barricade at the mouth of French Ending Street. We turned down another passage between buildings. I don't think anyone has ever run through the streets of Charleston as desperately as we did that night. It seemed that everything—curbs, streetposts, buildings—conspired to slow our progress; even the moon seemed vindictive, throwing up shadows, and making us misjudge distances. It constantly tripped us up as we ran along, and it kept rising. Dogs bayed dismally, but the eyes of cats were jewels that glittered mysteriously as we passed. We turned the corner and, with a sudden rush, a phosphorescence poured over the rooftops into the streets. We were stunned.

There was a knot of police at the corner. They looked back down at us.

We flattened ourselves against the side of a building.

Hirsch pulled himself through a window; Ned fell in after him, and I followed.

"Damn." I hit the shutter and it dissolved into splinters in the street.

We lay on our stomachs, panting, listening for sounds, wondering if we had been seen. I have no idea how long we were there, though it seemed eons. Our spasmodic breathing slowed, and I crawled to the window. "The coast is clear," I said. "You can get up." The police had disappeared. Looking the other way, I realized we were behind the whorehouse on Berresford Street where Hirsch and I used to meet. I felt odd. Maybe it was the moonlight sifting through the dark, or maybe it was the similar layout of rooms, but an eerie sense of dislocation, of unreality and reversal, came over me. It was as if we were suddenly transferred to the negative—what should have been dark was light in an obverse, mirrored world. Hirsch was still wearing Ned's clothes, and vice versa. Hess was confused with Grimke.

Slowly, so as not to make a sound, we went exploring like children in a haunted house. We could see there had once been luxury; we saw it in the flecked gilt and silk that came to dust in our fingers. Plaster medallions were platters of mold and fungus; plinths splintered like hopes and wallpaper peeled like dreams. As we moved through the rooms, dust shifted under our feet like silt at the bottom of the sea; cobwebs bantered like seaweed. Through the windows, we saw moonlight streaming in fractured patterns down the steps. We went through French doors into a ballroom. Ghost light spun, as above our heads, a chandelier cried one crystal prism tear. Hirsch held Ned's arm; he gave a hand motion, stopped, and listened. "Let's get out of here."

"What is it?" I asked. "The police?"

He shook his head. He stood there as if trying to remember something.

All old houses have their clinging memories. But this one

had it more than most. That ballroom was haunted with dreams. Just as we entered the oval mirrored room, a doorknob at its far end rattled, and a voice called out, "Is anyone here?"

We froze. We heard a click and a beam of light came through a crack between the locked doors. It hit a mirror and bounced at me. I ducked, and it followed. It slid over Ned's hand and just brushed Hirsch's cheek. It seemed a vindictive finger, accusing. It hovered around us for a while, but we were silent. It moved on into another room, and we sat back, relieved.

But Ned sneezed. The light came back, and bobbed insanely around the room.

"Run!" Hirsch cried, as he went scrambling across the parquet floor. We heard mirrors crack from behind us as we ran into the garden.

We ran to the walls, but they were too high to climb. We looked back through the trees that grew raggedly between us and the house. They had not been cared for in years, and we were assaulted with the tang of rot and the cloying scent of flowers. There was the smell of wisteria and lavender; the smell of passion and cedar permeated the air. It was black as pitch. We could see light moving behind the shutters and spilling out through the open doorway. We crawled under the bushes and hid.

In that garden, even with no wind, everything was stirring—each single branch a separate entity. Then, like a child, Ned piped up: "But Hirsch, we haven't done anything wrong. Why are we hiding?"

Hirsch hushed him.

"But Hirsch."

"You're queer, aren't you? That's enough; now shut up! Get yourself caught if you want to, but leave me alone."

There was a snap; I shut my eyes and put my face down on the ground. I barely breathed. Something was coming; and soon I could feel petals of flowers fall, blades of grass shiver, and piles of cracked leaves rustle. *It's here*, I thought. It came past me like a puff of wind and seemed a sort of energy. It changed us all. I know now that it was not a ghost, nor was it the police. They did not matter. It was really nothing more than our own moon love doubling back on us. The idea that we were damned and hunted like beasts took us like a chill. And in its wake, the world resumed. I could hear a cricket shrilling.

Hirsch was the first to stir. The idea had got him. No virus, vice, or virtue can be more impervious to healing. I opened my eyes just as the moon rose high between two chimneys, dispelling the darkness in the heart of the garden. I saw Hirsch rise. He stood in front of something I could not see.

I shut my eyes in prayer. I crouched, expecting the rush of feet and the thud of clubs.

"What is it?" Ned asked, crawling out from under his bush. I could hear them whispering.

I peeked: Hirsch was backing away from Ned's outstretched arms. "No," he was saying, as he shook his head. "Please." There was a look of horror on his face. "We're wrong," he said; "don't you see? They'll always be after us. We're queer." He was bright in moonlight, but threw his own shadow over Ned, who seemed to be absorbing the darkness just as Dah warned he would snatch the soul out of my body.

His energy flooded him. Hirsch stopped backing away from Ned, stopped, and looked at him. "It's you," Hirsch told him. "*You* made me believe." Moving toward him menacingly, he revealed what it was he had obscured from my sight: that eroded shapeless statue I had once glimpsed from our room on Berresford Street.

Hirsch kept approaching Ned, but now it seemed against his will. He tried to pull away, but the force, like that of a vacuum, was too strong for him. Ned stood there with his arms open to welcome him.

With a cry, Hirsch drew back sharply; he jerked and pushed by Ned, flinging him out of his way, throwing him off the walk, at the statue's feet. The breath was knocked out of Ned; and in a spray of gravel, Hirsch ran back to the house and into the street.

I bent to check on Ned as laughter rang out from the whorehouse; from beyond the glass-capped walls, rising higher than the wisteria, came a sudden discordant jazz note, and Ned, who had raised himself on his elbows to look after Hirsch, shook me off. He fell into his own shadows, sobbing.

✳

None of us dared to show up for work the next day. In fact, neither Ned nor Hirsch ever set foot again in the museum building. And when I went over to inquire of Hirsch the next week, Mrs. Hess told me he had left town. She was tight-lipped and would tell me nothing else. She twisted her hands and looked at me suspiciously. The next week, she and Mr. Hess disappeared, leaving their house on Mazyck Street empty and open. Although we made inquiries, we never found out where they went, just as I never told anyone of the dark accusations I had seen pass between Hirsch and Ned.

Maybe I should have, though. For then maybe Miss Wragg would not have blamed me for what happened to Ned Grimke.

ast night, after I came from the park, the bell began to ring. When I made it down, I had to squint to see the face of the boy at the door; the streetlight behind him blinded me. He just stared and said nothing. But he was not bad looking. He was afraid of me.

"Come on in, son," I said. He looked across the threshold apprehensively. I shuffled back up here and in a minute he followed. As I looked him up and down, he looked around, and I pointed him to a chair. When I told him I did not kill Ned, he looked at me, startled, as if I had read his mind.

"Well, that's why you're here, isn't it?"

He nodded.

"How did you find me?" I asked. "Miss Wragg?"

He did not answer. "Don't worry, I know she's the one who told you I'm guilty."

I pointed him to the bar and asked him to fix me a drink. He went up and obediently did so. He was dark and intense, and impossibly young.

I could tell by the cut of his clothes, the tilt of his nose, and even by the way he mixed my drink, that, like most of the boys who come here, he was from one of the very best families. They always are. They all live south of Broad Street (that street that is the boundary between longing and belonging). Their fathers are doctors or lawyers, their mothers no doubt in the Junior League. Those boys would stay put if they could, but their desires take them across respectable boundaries.

"Coming out," they call it today. Perhaps all the parents should hire Hibernian Hall, send out invitations, and, like the St. Cecilia Ball, devise an appropriate ceremony. But it's still what happened to Ned and Hirsch and me; still the stealth and shame and moonshade; it is the erotic ritual, that dance of desire gone through down at the Battery. If we look at them with lust, they are disgusted. Yet that is how they look at each other.

Those boys walk the streets that Ned and Hirsch and I walked, finding the old ideas, like old whores, still lingering with a venereal persistence. They take and are taken. When they wake, they blame, not themselves, but me.

They are afraid to know. Only I, an old man, an outsider, the Savannah puppeteer, can tell the truth, even though the bricks of Charleston's walls are old now, the mortar weak, and the secrets behind them seething. It's finally time to tell the truth about Hirsch Hess and Ned Grimke.

The boy last night told me he had already found traces of one of them in a second-hand store on King Street.

It was a piled and cluttered pawn shop of items unredeemed by the centuries. But what took the boy's eye most was an almost Chinese mask that dangled down from the pressed metal ceiling; tufts of hair straggled like seaweed from a face etched with agony.

"Oh, that's by Ned Grimke," the hunched little proprietor had told him. He showed the boy more masks, all detailed in torture. Looking through their eyes, the boy said, was like looking through a prism; he saw lesions painted in silver swirls and sores of paisley.

So he knew how Ned had felt, he said. But of Hirsch, he knew nothing.

"What happened to him?" the boy asked.

✳

I told him no one knows for sure, though some say he went to New York. Others are certain that he took his parents back to Europe and all were lost in that madness that came with Hitler out of Germany. I know he never came back to Charleston. (Some say he got married and presented his parents grandchildren.)

"But why did he leave Ned?" the boy wanted to know.

He was scared. And he was weak, not daring enough to go against what everyone else believed. None of us had the strength to go against our city.

✳

After Hirsch left, Ned knew what to do. After all, he had been brought up in the Confederate Home by old ladies who pressed relics and who warmed themselves with gone glory. So it was only natural that he clung to the one thing that Hirsch had left him: the idea that he was to blame, that he, not Hirsch, was guilty. It began to whittle at him; it hollowed him out; he began to dress and wear makeup like those other boys at the Peacock Alley. When the peephole opened and Chicco looked out, he saw a face like those masks the boy would discover later on King Street, marked less with fancy, looking more human and thus more frightening. Chicco was mad at Ned for driving Hirsch from town. So he eyed him coolly and his voice quavered with excitement when he said, "Get away from here."

Through the next few weeks, other doors were closing. Our colored maids lied for us, saying, "No, suh, he ain't here."

"How can we let him in?" Hilary asked. "If we did, he'd curse at us, or worse; he'd tell our parents." Ned had taken to going down the streets telling everyone he was queer. To save ourselves, we avoided him.

So Ned found other places. Dwin spotted him kneeling in front of some sailors at night in the Market. I passed him on Berresford Street. He was still wearing Hirsch's shirt. He smelled like sunned garbage and glared. He'd become a creature of the Battery.

BAM! ⟶ Without Hirsch, poor Ned was like a scholar with his theory. Step by step, he advanced upon his end. It was only logic, the idea, that drove him on, not the craving of a twisted psyche. And he found it so quickly that it made me think that the worst need not evolve, but that it is always there, just out of range, waiting. Powerless to stop it, I watched it pounce on Ned Grimke.

Stories soon rose in the black sections of town of a creature who whispered "love" to the returning fishermen as they walked up from the water. It was white, and it demanded a quarter; many were given eagerly. But when this vision lifted its cape, only bleached bones showed underneath.

Then, for a week, in the storefront theater by the navy base at the outskirts of town, there was talk of miracles. Enlisted men and ne'er-do-wells gathered. What they had come to leer at and pant over in moving pictures that flickered and fluttered uncertainly on the screen had become flesh and blood. But only for a week. Ned moved on, and his reputation, like a disease, was spreading throughout the city.

His trail was easy to follow and I followed him one night to Luden's house on High Battery. Inside, I found men willing to indulge a youngster in any of his fantasies. The pleasure/pain boundary was crossed so often that night that we obliterated it as easily as any line drawn in the sand.

There was an alcove under the eaves of the attic. The slatting reminded me of a cage. And in single file, one by one, we advanced upon it.

Ned was variegated by the light as a candle on the floor sent shadows along his body.

I suppose he had been at it for hours. He clutched piteously at men's thighs; he was after flesh like an addict;

his lips drooled and his eyes did not see. He called out deliriously.

There were men surrounding him. One lay beneath him; another was spreading his thighs; another bent over his face. The man writhed, sighed, and stood up. The next, standing to the right of me, pulled down his shorts and took his place.

Someone moved the candle so the light now touched Ned only when he rose into it. He seemed to be copulating with the shadows. That's the last time I saw Ned Grimke.

✳

The next day was Easter. My mother and I went to services at St. Michael's. The white church was blinding in the morning light.

Reverend Simkins' sermon had been somber and serene, especially considering what I had just seen; so I began to wonder if maybe the stories and words we recited were not real. I recited the prayers fervently, wanting to believe, until there was a ghastly draft on the back of my neck. Behind us a door opened; a murmur reached our ears.

I turned around to see an usher helping Azalea and Eola Grimke up the aisle. One whispered, "Sister, what is it?"

I could not concentrate after that. The words of our prayers were rolled on our tongues like pebbles worn down in a stream.

✳

That night, after church, everyone in town gossiped about the blood and Ned's disappearance. Someone had seen him after he left Luden's.

As if something had hooked him, "It's in me," he screamed. "It's in me!" But he would accept no help. "I'm queer," he said and laughed. He straightened up and started to sing an obscene ditty.

✳

They found his body three weeks later.

Miss Wragg took it the hardest. She wanted her own investigation and made references to me. It was logical, she said; it all came clear. She knew nothing of love, having only heard it in operas, seen it in plays, read it in stories. She did not know what we men could do to it; how we queers, feeling damned, could lacerate ourselves with it and bleed ourselves free.

She never accused me to my face. But Miss Richardson told me that my services were no longer needed as puppeteer. Miss Wragg never invited me back into her home.

God could forgive, but not Miss Wragg. She was sure I had done it in spite or jealousy. The word soon came from her drawing room that it was the "Savannah Puppeteer" who had killed Ned Grimke.

That's what the boy last night had heard. I'm sure he doubted me when I told him that Ned had left Luden's house soon after I did and went to the colored section of town.

In the black part of Charleston, like gateways to Hell, lamps light the mouths of allies. There is the glance, the gleam, faint laughter, and the sweat of bodies; and with one step in, the light is swallowed up and every further step is a voyage into mystery. I think it must have been in a razor fight over some stevedore that Ned was cut.

He dragged himself back to our part of town. He went into the garden of the Confederate Home. The next day, little red drops showed where he had been: to a bench under one of the porches, then to the staircase. The key, still in the keyhole, was bloody. He could have been saved, but he knew he did not deserve it. He had Hirsch's burden and knew he had to atone for all his sins as well as all those of the Peacock Alley.

✳

Three weeks later they found him. They said it was Ned, but how could they be sure that the disfigured and featureless thing that they had found floating off the Battery was really Ned Grimke?

I could not identify it. But Azalea and Eola did. They called Ned's father down from Walhalla and they all followed it to the cemetery. The granite stone over the grave just said, "Grimke."

For years I would go to the graveyard and look at it when I felt called to the Battery.

But it no longer suffices. For I was called down to the Battery again last night and saw that the moon still has men in its thrall and that there are men down there who, like Hirsch, blame, and those who, like Ned, believe. I came back here and wrote this down, hoping that you who read it will prevent the same thing from happening again.

But I'll be surprised if you do. For I myself have never been able to prevent anything, at least not since that summer day years ago when I tried to go against them and failed: my mother insisted and she surrendered me to Dah. I remember it was she who took me down the street to meet Ned Grimke.